THE AMAZING ADVENTURES OF

HARRY MOON

NOT YOUR BIRTHDAY BIRTHDAY

by

Mark Andrew Poe

with Barry Napier

Illustrations by Christina Weidman

rabbit publishers

Not Your Birthday Birthday (The Amazing Adventures of Harry Moon)
by Mark Andrew Poe
with Barry Napier
© Copyright 2017 by Mark Andrew Poe. All rights reserved.

Rabbit Publishers
1624 W. Northwest Highway
Arlington Heights, IL 60004

Illustrations by Christina Weidman
Interior Design by Lewis Design & Marketing
Creative Consultants: David Kirkpatrick, Thom Black, and Paul Lewis

ISBN: 978-1-943785-48-3

10 9 8 7 6 5 4 3 2 1

1. Fiction - Action and Adventure 2. Children's Fiction
First Edition
Printed in U.S.A.

"It's very special, isn't it?
Friendship."

~ *Rabbit*

TABLE OF CONTENTS

PROLOGUE

Halloween visited the little town of Sleepy Hollow and never left.

Many moons ago, a sly and evil mayor found the powers of darkness helpful in building Sleepy Hollow into "Spooky Town," one of the country's most celebrated attractions. Now, years later, a young eighth grade magician, Harry Moon, is chosen by the powers of light to do battle against the mayor and his evil consorts.

Welcome to *The Amazing Adventures of Harry Moon*. Darkness may have found a home in Sleepy Hollow, but if young Harry has anything to say about it, darkness will not be staying.

Family, Friends & Foes

Harry Moon

Harry is the thirteen-year-old hero of Sleepy Hollow. He is a gifted magician who is learning to use his abilities and understand what it means to possess the real magic.

An unlikely hero, Harry is shorter than his classmates and has a shock of inky, black hair. He loves his family and his town. Along with his friend Rabbit, Harry is determined to bring Sleepy Hollow back to its true and wholesome glory.

Rabbit

Now you see him. Now you don't. Rabbit is Harry Moon's friend. Some see him. Most can't.

Rabbit is a large, black-and-white, lop-eared, Harlequin rabbit. As Harry has discovered, having a friend like Rabbit has its consequences. Never stingy with advice and counsel, Rabbit always has Harry's back as Harry battles the evil that has overtaken Sleepy Hollow.

Honey Moon

She's a ten-year-old, sassy spitfire. And she's Harry's little sister. Honey likes to say she goes where she is needed, and sometimes this takes her into the path of danger.

Honey never gives in and never gives up when it comes to righting a wrong. Honey always looks out for her friends. Honey does not like that her town has been plunged into a state of eternal Halloween and is even afraid of the evil she feels lurking all around. But if Honey has anything to say about it, evil will not be sticking around.

III

Samson Dupree

Samson is the enigmatic owner of the Sleepy Hollow Magic Shoppe. He is Harry's mentor and friend. When needed, Samson teaches Harry new tricks and helps him understand his gift of magic.

Samson arranged for Rabbit to become Harry's sidekick and friend. Samson is a timeless, eccentric man who wears purple robes, red slippers, and a gold crown. Sometimes, Samson shows up in mysterious ways. He even appeared to Harry's mother shortly after Harry's birth.

Mary Moon

Strong, fair, and spiritual, Mary Moon is Harry and Honey's mother. She is also mother to two-year-old Harvest. Mary is married to John Moon.

Mary is learning to understand Harry and his destiny. So far, she is doing a good job letting Harry and Honey fight life's battles. She's grateful that Rabbit has come alongside to support and counsel her. But like all moms, Mary often finds it difficult to let her children walk their own paths. Mary is a nurse at Sleepy Hollow Hospital.

John Moon

John is the dad. He's a bit of a nerd. He works as an IT professional, and sometimes he thinks he would love it if his children followed in his footsteps. But he respects that Harry, Honey, and possibly Harvest will need to go their own way. John owns a classic sports car he calls Emma.

Titus Kligore

Titus is the mayor's son. He is a bully of the first degree but also quite conflicted when it comes to Harry. The two have managed to forge a tentative friendship, although Titus will assert his bully strength on Harry from time to time.

Titus is big. He towers over Harry. But in a kind of David vs. Goliath way, Harry has learned which tools are best to counteract Titus's assaults while most of the Sleepy Hollow kids fear him. Titus would probably rather not be a bully, but with a dad like Maximus Kligore, he feels trapped in the role.

Maximus Kligore

The epitome of evil, nastiness, and greed, Maximus Kligore is the mayor of Sleepy Hollow. To bring in the cash, Maximus turned the town into the nightmarish, Halloween attraction it is today.

He commissions the evil-tinged celebrations in town. Maximus is planning to take Sleepy Hollow with him to Hell. But will he? He knows Harry Moon is a threat to his dastardly ways, but try as he might, he has yet to rid himself of Harry's meddling.

Kligore lives on Folly Farm and owns most of the town, including the town newspaper.

An Underground Meeting

Six hundred sixty-six feet below the surface of the tiny town of Sleepy Hollow, six figures huddled around an elaborate conference table. The table was made of ancient oak and sat in the center of a boardroom that was not a room at all but a cavern known as the Underground Grotto. The walls were made of stone. In the corner of the cavern, a fire roared from a large stone hearth heating the place even though it was plenty hot without it.

The Grotto was located directly beneath Folly Farm, owned by Mayor Maximus Kligore. More precisely, the Grotto was exactly beneath the Kligore mansion, connected by an elevator shaft embedded in old caves, mines, and tunnels that had never seen the light of day. Beyond all of that dark dirt and rock, the Grotto seemed to be carved almost naturally out of the earth.

At the head of the table was Mayor Maximus Kligore. To his right was his faithful minion, Oink. His minion was a terrible-looking hound who wasn't really a hound at all, but a beast of the Underworld. On the opposite side of the table from Oink sat two tall figures that wore dark robes. Their faces were covered in the shadows of their cowls. The Mayor knew them only as The Quiet Ones, assistants of B.L. Zebub. They attended any meeting affecting the business dealings of the We Drive By Night Company.

At the other end of the table sat a tall, thin woman. The chair seemed to mold itself around her body. Her long, purple hair faded into midnight black by the time it reached her waist. This was Lady Dra Dra, the Imperial Captain of Dragons. She reported directly to B.L. Zebub. Like The Quiet Ones, she was usually in attendance at any major meetings.

Still, the most important member of this particular meeting was sitting at the mayor's right hand. It was Marcus Kligore, the mayor's oldest son. He was well dressed with dark hair and dark eyes. He had just turned seventeen. The time had come to find out what role he would play in the always expanding We Drive By Night Company.

"I must say," Lady Dra Dra remarked, slinking like a snake in the comfort of her chair. "Mr. Zebub has been only moderately satisfied with We Drive By Night's progress as of late. We certainly hope that the official addition of Marcus may help move our cause along."

"There *have* been obstacles," Mayor Kligore

said. "But we have never given up. Sleepy Hollow is forever in the palm of my hand."

"Yes, only one gloomy, little town," Lady Dra Dra said. "But we can do so much more with the rest of the world. That is, of course, the ultimate plan."

"Mr. Zebub knows about our most daunting foe, correct?" Mayor Kligore asked.

Lady Dra Dra smiled. "Yes, indeed. Harry Moon. A mere boy. Hardly anything to set us back."

"He's more than just a boy," Oink interjected. "He has the sort of magic that we have never been able to stop."

"We are all aware of Harry Moon's skills and his tendency to meddle in our affairs," Lady Dra Dra said. "Mr. Zebub is keeping an eye on the boy. But I am not going to waste our valuable time tonight speaking about a puny, little thirteen-year-old child. Instead, we want to focus on how Marcus could help take We Drive

By Night to the next level. And I believe I have the answer."

Everyone in the Grotto leaned forward, even The Quiet Ones. The body language of the dark figures showed keen interest. But no one listened with more anticipation than Marcus Kligore. He had been waiting for this day for as long as he could walk. It was time to make his father proud . . . to take part in the work of his father's life.

5

"Well, what is it?" the mayor asked.

"Birthdays," Lady Dra Dra answered.

"Birthdays?" said the mayor, Marcus, and Oink all at once.

Lady Dra Dra smirked. "Of course. Birthdays. It's perfect. If you knew as much as you like to think you do, you'd all know that birthdays are by far the biggest holiday the dark side has working for it."

"But a birthday is not a holiday," Mayor

Kligore countered.

"Well, no, not in terms of a calendar," Lady Dra Dra said. She leaned forward and smiled sinisterly at the other five figures. "But think about it. The highest of all holidays for We Drive By Night is one's own birth. This is because the birthday is all about *you*. This one day is our best opportunity to attract new clients.

"On birthdays, the one doing the celebrating receives heaps and gobs of self-absorbed praise for no reason other than turning a year older. It's a huge confidence boost and leads to massively inflated egos. And people with egos can be . . . well, *useful* to us."

Mayor Kligore smiled. "Of course, of course," he said, as if he had already thought of this but had been keeping it a secret all along. "But how do you plan to capture that self-satisfaction in a way that can benefit us rather than simply making humans feel better about themselves?"

"As usual, Mr. Zebub has already structured it for you," Lady Dra Dra said. "We will set

Marcus to be in charge of a new business—a party business that will be known as Birthday Fantasies, a subsidiary of the We Drive by Night Company."

"In charge of a business?" Marcus asked in a spoiled, whiny tone. "That sounds like a lot of work."

"Of course it is, you sniveling, spoiled snot," Lady Dra Dra said. "Your lazy days of partying and charming ladies are over. Or, at least, taking a temporary pause. You've wanted to worm your way into the family business, and this is your ticket. Like everything else in your rotten existence, it's being handed to you on a plate."

"But what sort of business specializes in birthdays?" the mayor asked.

"The sort of business that specializes in feeding the human ego," Lady Dra Dra said. "It's genius, really. You never run out of customers because everyone has a birthday. And when you think about how much money and passion parents put into birthday parties for their gross, little, cretin children, it's a surefire success just waiting to happen."

"We could do themed parties," Marcus said, suddenly interested. "I could plan the parties and make them awesome."

"That's the spirit," Lady Dra Dra said, smiling at Marcus in a way that would have made any other young man weak in the knees.

"As far as details go, there aren't many. Birthday Fantasies will be a one-stop shop. Fantasies will buy all the decorations and provide the venue and entertainment. We Drive By Night, in turn, will take the profit."

"Oh, this is fantastic," Mayor Kligore said. "When can we start?"

"We already have," she answered.

She clicked her fingers, and a spark leaped out of the fireplace. It landed in the center of the table. In a bright flash, the flame was gone, leaving a sheet of paper in its place. It was a flier, elaborately decorated with balloons and fancy masks. Tendrils of smoke licked up from its edges. In the center, in large block letters, it read—

BIRTHDAY FANTASIES!

Because you deserve the very best on your special day!

Parties of all shapes and sizes, for all ages!

Start planning for your BIG DAY right away!

Call BIRTHDAY FANTASIES today at 666-4247

9

"These will be posted all over Sleepy Hollow tomorrow," Lady Dra Dra said. "And after Sleepy Hollow, we'll expand."

Oink stood up in his chair, drooling over the flier. "This is going to be great!"

Marcus snatched the flier from the hound and drew it close to him. "Oh, I don't think I'll need your help," he said. "You stupid, bumbling creature."

"Already thinking he's in control, I see," Lady Dra Dra commented. "Just like his father."

"Yes, well," Mayor Kligore said, "this is a fabulous idea, and I can assure you that we will make it a success."

Lady Dra Dra stood up from her chair and stretched. She looked impossibly tall, her legs and arms getting lost in the shadows of the room. "I hope for your sake, you're right."

With that, she walked to the fire, bent down, and walked directly into it. The flames hugged

her for a moment, as if they, too, could appreciate her sleek beauty. Then with a fizzle of smoke, she disappeared.

The Quiet Ones stood next, and each one of them took a position by the Grotto's exit. This, the mayor knew, was a sign that this meeting was over. He got up, motioning for Marcus and Oink to do the same.

The Quiet Ones ushered them out of the Grotto and down a large cavern that stopped at an ancient, wooden elevator that was made of chains, pulleys, and a simple wooden box. The Kligores and their servant stepped into the old elevator, and the Quiet Ones closed the thick wooden door, bolting it shut from the outside.

"Does it always have to be this dramatic?" Marcus asked, looking around the old, wooden, crank-operated elevator with disgust.

"For goodness sake, son," Mayor Kligore said. Marcus rolled his eyes at his father but then looked at the flier he still held in his hands. He smiled at the flier with pride. It was still warm from its departure from the fire.

"Can't you take something serious for once?" asked his father.

"You know, Dad," he replied, "I think I can."

MAGIC SHOW BLUES

Harry Moon placed his magic hat and wand carefully into his case, snapped the lid closed, and looked back out to the birthday party. Everyone seemed to still be wowed by the show he had just put on. A few guys were still talking about how he'd made Rabbit disappear, reappear, and then bark like a dog. Personally, though,

Harry's favorite trick was having someone select a card from his deck and then have the card appear in the person's underpants.

A happy crowd was very important to Harry. He liked to know that his magic made people happy, but more than that, a happy crowd meant good word of mouth. And if people were spreading good reviews about his magic shows, that meant he'd be more likely to get booked for another magic show—usually at birthday parties.

With his case packed up, he went into the living room where the partygoers were still talking about his magic show.

"What an awesome show," said Marty, a sixth grader he barely knew.

"How did you do that thing with the rabbit?" asked another kid.

"Finding that nine of spades in my underpants was no fun," moaned Douglas Pincher, the birthday boy. He turned eleven today, and even though he *had* seemed displeased to find the playing card in his underpants, he still appeared to have had a great time.

"Well," Harry said, "happy birthday, Douglas.

15

I hope it's fantastic!"

With that, Harry made his way into the Pincher family's kitchen where Mrs. Pincher was slicing up the birthday cake and doling it out onto paper plates.

"I'm all done, Mrs. Pincher," Harry said.

"Oh, great," she replied. She set her knife down and reached into her pocket. "Here's your payment. And I must say, it was well deserved. I'll be telling all of my friends about your wonderful magic show!"

"Thanks," Harry said, smiling.

Mrs. Pincher handed him a fifty dollar bill, which Harry pocketed quickly. He knew he could get more for his services; after all, there were two balloon artists in town that charged three hundred dollars per party and a not-too-funny clown that charged four hundred. And if you wanted bouncy houses for your kid's party in Sleepy Hollow, you could expect to spend almost an even thousand.

Harry was glad to be able to offer an affordable alternative. Honestly, he loved magic so much that he'd do the shows for free. But he was a very busy thirteen-year-old, saving for his college fund, and knew that having some extra money was always a good thing. Harry wasn't a spoiled kid at all, and John and Mary Moon had taught him that saving money for the future was one of the wisest thing a kid his age could do.

"Would you like some cake before you go?" Mrs. Pincher asked him.

"No, thanks."

"Are you sure? It's chocolate chip ice cream cake."

Harry paused at the door and turned back into the kitchen. Yes, he was a responsible thirteen-year-old, but there are very few responsibilities that win out over ice cream cake.

Harry returned home that Saturday afternoon with a stomach filled with ice cream cake and punch. He was feeling a little sluggish, but with a crisp, new fifty dollar bill in his pocket, it was hard to feel down. He set his case down in his room and changed out of his magician robes. Once he was dressed, he noticed that his good friend, confidant, and sometimes disappearing assistant, Rabbit, was sitting on the edge of his bed.

"Great show today, Harry," he said.

"Thanks, Rabbit. You were spot-on as always."

"Thanks. But really . . . barking like a dog? I can do much better. I can speak Latin, you know."

"You can?" Harry asked.

"Yes, indeed. I really feel that we aren't exploring my talents enough in these shows."

"We'll work something out for next time," Harry said, grinning.

Satisfied, Rabbit twitched his whiskers.

As Harry was about to open up his laptop and go online to find some new tricks to practice, he heard a high-pitched squealing sound from downstairs. It was obviously the squeal of Honey Moon, his younger sister. She was excited about something . . . an emotion she rarely showed as she was usually too busy thumbing her nose at Harry and their younger brother, Harvest.

Harry and Rabbit looked at one another quizzically. Harry shrugged and then headed downstairs to see what all of the excitement was about.

He found Honey sitting at the table with a piece of mail in her hand. The torn pink envelope was on the table while the contents—a glittery card with flowery writing—was gripped firmly in her hand.

John and Mary Moon had also come into the kitchen. They had looks of alarm on their faces as if they thought the squeals had been from pain or fear.

"My goodness," Mary Moon said. "What's all of the excitement about?"

Honey flashed the card at her parents and leaped down from her chair, jumping with excitement. "I got an invitation to Malory Marvel's birthday party! And it's *princess themed!*"

"Didn't Malory have a birthday party two weekends ago?" Honey's mom asked.

"No, Mom," Honey said. "That was Judy Sorenson."

"Oh, they all run together."

"And don't forget," Harry said, "that I've got Declan's birthday party tomorrow."

"What?" John Moon said. "*Another* birthday party?"

"Yes," Mary Moon said. "I remembered that one. Have you got a gift yet, Harry?"

"No, not yet. I figured I'd pick something up

20

tomorrow after church on the way to the party."

"Well, I'm not going to make you pay with your own money. That wouldn't be fair to you. We'll give you some money for a gift."

"Thanks," Harry said.

"Well then," Mary Moon said, walking to the dry-erase calendar on the fridge. "Looks like another entry into the calendar. This is shaping up to be a busy month."

Harry looked at the calendar and saw that she was right. With Declan's party tomorrow and Malory Marvel's the week after that, the Moon kids (even including little Harvest who, really, had no friends yet) had five birthday parties to attend.

"So," Honey said, still ogling the card as if it were some great treasure. "Can I RSVP to this?"

"Yes," Mary Moon said.

Mary Moon tried to be cheerful, but Harry could tell that something was bothering her—and it didn't take a great magician to see that.

TOO MANY BIRTHDAYS

When the kids were in bed, John and Mary Moon took up their respective places in the living room. They sat side by side on the couch, John's arm wrapped lovingly around Mary. Sometimes they watched television, but Saturdays usually wore them out. They'd both planned to be in bed by ten o' clock that night, so in the morning, they wouldn't be rushed to get to church on time.

"You okay, dear?" John asked Mary. "You seem troubled."

"It's nothing serious," Mary said. "It's just that this birthday party nonsense is getting out of hand. When did *everyone* start having a party?"

"There *have* been a lot of them lately, haven't there?" John asked.

24

"Yes. They always seem to sneak up on us. I'm starting to really think we need to budget extra money for birthday presents."

"What do we spend on presents?" John asked.

Mary, who did all of the birthday shopping, thought for a moment. "Well, usually around fifty dollars per child. So this month alone, we'll be spending two hundred and fifty dollars on birthday presents."

"What?!" John Moon exclaimed. "That's outrageous. Surely we can spend less, right?"

"Of course. But then our own children start to feel pressured, you know? They feel that they have to give great gifts to match the expensive presents everyone else is giving."

"That's nonsense," John said. "When I was a child, I was lucky to get a birthday card with a crusty, old dollar bill in it."

"Times are different now," Mary said.

"Boy, are they ever!"

"Kids are only kids once, I suppose," she said. "Think about our own children. They're good kids. They deserve to be spoiled every now and then . . . don't they?"

"Not with fifty dollar gifts from all of their friends on their birthdays!"

"Hmm," Mary Moon said. This was her solemn little sound of agreement.

They fell quiet after that as the Moon household watched another day draw to a close. As John and Mary Moon got up from the couch and headed for their bedroom, neither of them heard the slight creaking of the stairs nor the feet of one of their children retreating back to their bedroom.

Harry had heard the whole conversation. He'd gotten up to use the bathroom and had heard his mother sighing. She'd said something

about a birthday and Harry wondered if it had something to do with Declan's party tomorrow. He quietly dashed to the stairway, headed down a few steps, and listened in.

But instead of hearing anything about tomorrow's party, he heard his mother's concerns over the insane number of birthday parties they were subjected to.

Two hundred fifty dollars! It seemed crazy to Harry. He wondered how many birthday parties he and Honey attended in the course of a year. Right off of the top of his head, Harry could think of fifteen that he went to every year without fail. Honey also had ten regulars, maybe more. And there were a few here and there that they got invited to unexpectedly.

That's a lot of money, Harry thought. It astounded him. Suddenly the fifty bucks he'd been paid for the Pincher birthday party seemed very small.

When he heard his parents get up from the

couch, he bounded quietly up the stairs and back into his room. He lay down on his bed, a feeling of guilt starting to gnaw at him.

"You there, Rabbit?" he asked into the darkness.

"You know it," Rabbit said.

"Were you sleeping?"

Rabbit only chuckled. Harry was pretty sure his magical friend never slept.

"What's bothering you?" Rabbit asked.

"Do you think having birthday parties is selfish?"

"Oh, that's a very good question, Harry. I think it depends on why you have the party. Some have them to get gifts. Others have them to be around their friends. And honestly, some have them just because their parents make them; it becomes a social affair for the parents more than a celebration for the children."

Harry had been to a few of those parties. Actually, he'd been to all three kinds that Rabbit had just described. He *had* always gotten a selfish vibe from some of them. Some of the parties he performed magic at had made him feel out of place—like he had only been there to make the party more unique just so some kid could feel like he was better than everyone else.

As he drifted off to sleep, Harry decided that he was going to tell his parents that he never wanted another birthday party. He was also going to be very selective about the parties he attended—just Hao, Bailey, and Declan's parties, probably. They were all part of the Good Mischief Team, so their parties were a must.

29

Besides . . . the best part about going to most birthday parties was for the ice cream and cake. And he could get plenty of that by performing magic at other kids' parties.

It was just one of the many perks of being a kid magician.

30

BIRTHDAY FANTASIES

As Lady Dra Dra had said, the fliers for Birthday Fantasies had been plastered around town. Within a day, they even had a building with an elaborate sign out front. It was easily one of the most colorful business signs in Sleepy Hollow; it was so bright that it could be seen from two blocks away.

The building itself was no less elaborate. The storefront was on Magic Row and was without a doubt the newest business on the block. The windows were clean whereas the other shop windows on Magic Row were dusty with age, giving them an antique and charming sort of vibe. But not Birthday Fantasies—no, this place was making it no secret that it was the hip, new place in town. Neon lights traced the roof and a mural of balloons, streamers, and Greek masks were painted on the side.

Inside, business was already booming. The place was small but bustling. Even after only a week in business, they had managed to book themselves solid for the next two weeks. Marcus Kligore had an office. Oink manned the front desk, usually in a not-too-convincing receptionist's outfit.

Of course, Marcus could not always be there because he was still in school. But so far, for the one week they had been open for business,

he had managed to speak with each and every client. Today, a Sunday, was shaping up to be promising. They had a party booked—their third of the weekend—and word was quickly spreading about how awesome a Birthday Fantasies birthday party could be.

Shortly before noon on that Sunday, Mayor Kligore stepped into the Birthday Fantasies office. There was a spring of excitement in his step that made Oink smile from behind the desk. On the wall was a calendar listing all of the parties that they had already booked for the coming weeks.

Mayor Kligore headed straight for Marcus's office and closed the door behind him. His eldest son was sitting behind his desk, busily typing something into his laptop.

"A busy day today, yes?" the mayor asked.

"Oh yeah," Marcus said. "I've got a thirteen-year-old's party in an hour and someone's twenty-first birthday at seven o' clock this evening."

"Splendid! Is there anything I can do?"

"Nope. I've got it all covered."

"You're sure? You've never been given such responsibility before."

Marcus rolled his eyes and stopped typing. He looked up at his father and frowned. "We've already thrown two parties, and they went over very well. The bacon-themed one was amazing—although I don't think Oink enjoyed it much."

Mayor Kligore eyed his son suspiciously. It was nice to see the kid behind a desk, in an office trying to take charge of everything. It seemed to suit him well. Even if he still had one year remaining of high school, Marcus Kligore was already carving up the world to suit his needs . . . and the future of the We Drive By Night Company.

Still, it was hard to believe that this young man—whom he still thought of as a kid, really—was so close to stepping into the real world. It was even harder to believe that he was less than a year from being done with high school and being able to fully commit to furthering the reign of We Drive By Night.

"Very well, then," Mayor Kligore said. "I see you have it all under control. But you know that you can call on me when you need help, right?'

"Right-o, Dad-o."

They fell silent, simply looking at one another. The awkward quiet was broken by the ringing of Marcus's cell phone. "Sorry, got to take this," Marcus said, snapping his phone up.

35

"See you later, son," the Mayor said.

Marcus barely even gave a wave as he answered the call, and his father walked out of the office, both proud and uneasy.

Marcus was preparing for the afternoon

party, thinking about his father's weird visit earlier in the day. He couldn't help but think that his father did not trust him. And while that hurt a bit, Marcus understood it. He was known around Sleepy Hollow for being something of a slacker—but a dashingly handsome and well-dressed slacker. He was the guy that attended parties, and when he arrived, the parties instantly became more fun.

Marcus Kligore, according to just about anyone in Sleepy Hollow, had been born with a silver spoon in his mouth (albeit a rather jagged and mysterious spoon) and had never taken the time to do anything for himself. He was nothing more than the funny guy that sometimes messed everything up . . . but that didn't matter because his daddy would always take care of it.

In other words, nobody ever took him seriously. But as far as Marcus was concerned, running Birthday Fantasies was his chance to change all of that. He was taking this seriously. He'd prove to his father that he could be responsible. More than that, he'd also impress Lady Dra Dra and the never-seen, yet no less intimidating, B.L. Zebub. And he'd do it by milking this crummy little town for all it was worth.

These themed birthday parties required a

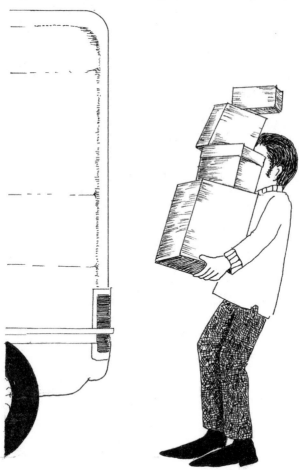

huge upfront fee, and the parents of all the spoiled Sleepy Hollow kids were more than willing to fork their cash over. The best part of all was the more popular Birthday Fantasies became, the more he could charge. Dreams of wealth at any cost pulsed through his body. He had learned from his father that greed was not bad. Greed was good.

They were already taking calls for party bookings at least four times a day!

With these thoughts galloping through his head, Marcus loaded up the Birthday Fantasies van with boxes of decorations, costumes, and goodie bags for the afternoon party. Sure, it was just some lame ninja-themed party for a thirteen-year-old, but it had the potential to be epic.

I'll show Dad, Marcus thought as he headed out for the party. *I'll show all of them!*

It made him feel more grown up to be manning this party on his own. Sure, Oink and Ug would be there later to help, but even then, he was the man in charge. It was a great feeling and made him realize why his father enjoyed being the mayor of Sleepy Hollow so much.

Marcus was quickly finding that power was easy to get used to. And he couldn't wait until Birthday Fantasies had overtaken the town, growing into a larger company that would be able to stretch its power out into the rest of the country and, eventually, the world.

39

40

PARTY TIME!

When Harry Moon stepped into the front door of Declan's house, his eyes went wide. The house was decked out in some of the most elaborate decorations Harry had ever seen. He'd known that Declan had planned a ninja-themed party, but he had not been expecting the house to look so awesome.

It appeared to be an authentic Japanese dojo. The floors had been covered with what looked like real bamboo mats, and the windows had been covered with some sort of clear paneling that made Harry feel like he had stepped directly into a kung-fu movie.

Mrs. Dickinson met him at the door and handed him an outfit from a box. Harry looked at it and saw that it was an authentic karate uniform. Because Declan was very heavily involved in all things ninja, Harry knew that this outfit was usually referred to as a gi.

"Just slip it on over your clothes if you want," Mrs. Dickinson said. "Or feel free to change in the bathroom. The other boys are already downstairs in the basement."

"Thanks," Harry said. He then showed her

the present his family had rushed to pick up after church. He's only been able to wrap it in a gift bag. "What do I do with the present?"

"On the kitchen table, please."

Harry took his gi and the present to the kitchen. When he set his gift bag on the table, he saw the massive heap of presents and thought about the money that must have gone into all of them. The conversation he'd overheard between his parents was still heavy on his heart as he walked away from the table and into the bathroom to change.

He was pleased with the way the gi fit him, and he really did feel like a real ninja with it on—even though he knew absolutely nothing about karate. He bounded down the stairs to the Dickinson's basement and joined ten other boys decked out in identical gis. The only gi that was different was Declan's. His was red and black while the other boys had white and black ones.

There were two entertainers in the middle

43

of the group of boys, also dressed in karate garb. One of them was holding a chunk of thick wood while the other approached it, making a fist against it. Harry watched, fascinated, as the entertainer drew his hand back and shattered the board in half.

44

"No way!" Hao said.

"That was *awesome!*" Bailey said.

"How'd you . . . how did he . . . ?" asked a stupefied Clooney Mackay.

"Karate takes great discipline," one of the entertainers said, "but also, great fun! So go at it!"

In a ferocious commotion, all eleven boys in attendance went for one another. They all pretended to attack, thrusting out lazy kicks and punches. It was all in good fun and even Harry found himself getting involved. After a while, the entertainers brought out a box of foam-covered weapons: nunchakus, fake swords, and other things of which Harry didn't even know the names.

It did not take very long before all of the boys were sweating. The pretend battle broke up as most of them headed upstairs for something to drink. Harry and Bailey were preoccupied with an epic foam-sword fight, which they decided to call a draw. They were the last two boys remaining in the basement and hurried up after the others. As Harry made his way to the stairs, tossing his fake sword into the pile of other harmless weapons, he spotted the two party entertainers standing along the far side of the room, digging through another box with party props.

Harry paused, looking hard at one of the men. There was something about the man that struck Harry as odd. He looked stout but was also hunched over slightly. The way the man stood upright and had to hunch to bend over to peer into the box made Harry think of a man on stilts. It was then, as the man leaned into the box, that the black headband he had been wearing slid slightly along the side of his head.

What Harry saw made him understand what had seemed so off about the entertainer.

He was not a man at all—proven by the large, floppy ear that hung over the headband and the slightly mottled skin sitting beneath what was clearly a wig of black hair.

It was Oink!

46

The fun of the staged ninja battle was suddenly forgotten. Harry knew that wherever Oink was, there was sure to be trouble. *But really, what was Oink doing at a birthday party? More than that, why was he trying to act like a skilled ninja?*

Harry ran up the stairs behind Declan, wondering if Oink had noticed that he was there. When he joined the other boys for juice and water, he took a closer look at the decorations. He wondered if Oink himself was somehow involved with the party. What other reason would he have to be here? Was Oink working part time for a birthday party planner?

That didn't seem right. Unless the We Drive By Night Company was behind this. He broke away from the group of boys, feeling that he needed to get out of there.

"Sorry, guys," Harry said to his pals. "I need to head out. I don't . . . I don't feel so good."

He ran down the hall. As he did, his eyes

landed once again on the table filled with presents. They all seemed almost sinister now that he knew they had been brought to a party that was somehow tied to the mayor and his goons.

As he reached the door, Declan and Bailey also came into the hall.

"Yo, Harry-san," Declan said. "Are you okay? You not enjoying the party?"

48

"No, I really am. It's a great party," Harry said. "It's just . . . I don't know. This headache came out of *nowhere*."

He hated lying, especially to his friends, but he really didn't feel like getting deep into his worries right now. There was no point in ruining his friends' good time. "Well, that stinks," Bailey said. "I hope it's nothing serious."

"Yeah," Harry said, thinking about Oink in the basement downstairs. "Me neither."

ACCIDENTS HAPPEN

"Hey, Harry!"

Harry hadn't even made it to the end of the block before he heard someone call his name. He turned around and saw Hao riding his bike toward him.

"What are you doing?" Harry asked, confused as to why Hao had also left the party.

"I had to leave early," Hao said. "What about you?"

"Oh, I'm not feeling too well," Harry fibbed.

"That's no good," Hao sympathized.

"Why are you leaving early?"

"I've got to be at work in half an hour."

"Oh, at the Screaming Jelly Bean?" Harry asked.

"No, this job is at the recreation center over on Moon Lake."

"So you switched jobs?"

"No, I still work at the Screaming Jelly Bean. I also get a few hours in over at Saywell's Drugstore. The job at Moon Lake just started last week."

"You have three jobs?" Harry exclaimed.

"Yeah. They're all part-time, though."

"Still . . . you're fourteen and in school. How do you find the time to do it all?"

Hao smiled, rather proud of himself. "It's tricky. But I need the money. Mom tries really hard, you know? But things like these birthday parties mean more money. And we don't have a lot, so I have to do my part."

51

Harry nodded. He sometimes forgot that Hao didn't have a father. Harry had never heard the whole story, but he thought Hao's dad had not been around since Hao was three years old or so. His mom worked two jobs, and sometimes Harry noticed Hao's meager packed lunches at school, often just a peanut butter and jelly sandwich.

"That's actually very cool of you," Harry said. "I wish I had a job."

"You do! You're a magician."

"Oh yeah," Harry said. Sometimes he didn't think of his magic shows as jobs. He had way too much fun with them to consider them any form of work.

"It's helped me realize how much money mom used to spend to make sure I had birthday presents for all of my friend's parties," Hao said.

"So you pay for all of your own gifts now?"

Harry asked.

"Yeah," Hao said. "And let me tell you, it really adds up. That's why I have three jobs."

The boys walked together across the next block, and Harry's thoughts once again turned to seeing Oink at Declan's birthday party. He couldn't shake the feeling that Mayor Kligore was up to no good, as usual.

But how could he possibly cause harm by creating a company that helped put on awesome birthday parties?

"Well," Hao said, straddling his bike and breaking Harry's train of thought. "I need to get going if I'm going to make it to work on time."

"Okay," Harry said. "Have fun and drive safe."

Hao gave a small wave before pumping at the pedals of his bike and taking off with surprising speed. Harry watched him go,

53

returning the wave and rather in awe of his friend. Three jobs, Harry thought. I can't even imagine!

Harry continued to hurry home. Maybe the mayor wasn't up to anything evil, but Harry felt like he needed to do some investigating just to be sure.

54

One of the things Hao was known for among his friends was his ability to get his bike to go so fast that the chain whined musically against the chain guard. It made that exact music as he blazed his bike down Paul Revere Avenue. Declan's house was on the exact opposite side of town from Moon Lake. It was about two miles in all, and he had to get there in fifteen minutes. He knew he could do it and was happy for any excuse to get his bike to hit its top speed.

Hao loved his bike. He knew it had to be the fastest in Sleepy Hollow. He'd even given it the name of the Lean, Mean, Speed Machine.

He took the curb at the intersection of Paul Revere and Main Street in a flash. A few adults gave him scornful looks while some of the younger kids looked at him in awe like he was a superhero. He jetted around the edge of the town square (which was really a circle shape—just one of Sleepy Hollow's weird little quirks), smiling as the breeze swept his hair back. For just a moment, he stopped pedaling, closed his eyes, and pretended that he was flying.

He opened his eyes quickly when a beeping horn sounded out from nearby. He was nearing another intersection and rather than stop, he wheeled hard down the street, snuck in behind traffic, and crossed the road.

He wondered what everyone was doing at Declan's party right now. He had hated to leave early, but he really wanted to impress Mr. Spookston, the manager at the Moon Lake rec center. If he could hold on to this job and keep Mr. Spookston happy all the way through high school, he'd always have some extra money in his pocket.

With his chain still singing by his feet, Hao guided the Lean, Mean, Speed Machine onto Conical Hat Avenue. Hao saw nothing but empty road ahead of him. He knew that cutting straight across the street and winding through the back lots of a few stores would get him to Moon Lake faster than staying on his current route. His shortcut would shave five minutes off of his time.

Of course, he had to cross the road to do that—something he was not supposed to do unless he was at a traffic light and he had the right of way. But he figured this one time wouldn't hurt anything. The streets were pretty empty because it was Sunday afternoon, and he really needed to get to work on time.

With a quick glance in both directions, Hao turned sharply and barreled out into Conical Hat Avenue. He pedaled harder, making sure to get to the other side as quickly as possible.

Out of nowhere, the constant music of his bike chain was drowned out by another blaring

horn.

Hao heard the screeching of tires and turned to his right just in time to see the car before it struck his bike's back wheel. He let out a quick scream as his bike was turned sideways. Hao flew from the seat, catapulted hard to the right. The world seemed to float away for a moment and then reintroduced itself as Hao slammed into the sidewalk. The wind went rushing out of him in a mighty oooof, but that was the least of his worries.

71

He also heard a sharp snap that sent a jolt of horrible pain through his leg. Hao cried out again, reaching down for his leg but unable to grab it. He was barely aware of someone getting out of the car that had struck him. It was a woman, rushing to him and saying something in a high, panic-filled voice.

"Oh my goodness, are you okay?" the woman asked, kneeling by his side.

"Huh," Hao said. "Sorry. Was trying to get to work and . . ."

But the pain in his leg was far too much for him to bear. He blinked up at the woman one final time, saw the Lean, Mean, Speed Machine sprawled on the road a few feet away, and then blacked out.

THEM'S THE BREAKS

Because his mother was a full-time nurse, Harry Moon had been in and out of Sleepy Hollow Hospital and Urgent Care. He'd also occupied a bed within the hospital a few times—perhaps a few more times than a usually safe thirteen-year-old kid should. So visiting the hospital was not really scary for him.

But what made him feel so uncomfortable later that night when his mother pulled up to the visitor parking lot of Sleepy Hollow Hospital, was the idea of seeing Hao all banged up. Now, with a friend injured inside, the hospital was more than just some place where his mom worked. Now it looked sinister.

Bailey and Declan sat in the back seat. He was sitting in the passenger seat. It was nine o' clock at night. It was too late to be out on a school night, but Harry's mom had made an exception, as had Declan and Bailey's mothers.

They'd all received a phone call from Hao's mother around six o' clock that afternoon. She had informed them that Hao had been struck by a car while riding his bike to work. He had broken his leg in the accident but seemed to be okay otherwise. Once the leg had been reset and placed in a cast, Hao had been taken to a room where doctors wanted to keep the leg elevated and make sure the medicine they were giving him for his pain was taking hold. It looked like he might be staying overnight.

Still, as soon as he was in his room, Hao had asked to see his friends. And that was why Mary Moon had volunteered to drive the other members of the Good Mischief Team to the hospital at such a late hour.

"You boys want me to come in with you?" Mary asked.

"No, thanks, Mom," Harry said.

"Yeah, but thanks for the ride," Bailey said as the boys piled out of the car.

61

"Don't stay too long," Mary Moon said. "It's getting late, and Hao will need his rest."

Together, the three boys walked into the hospital. Harry was starting to feel weirded out about how the place was making him feel. He'd marched through the entrance lobby and rode the elevators countless times. But now everything about the hospital made him feel uneasy—the smell, the way-too-clean layout of it all, and even the way the receptionist at the desk smiled at them.

Apparently, Bailey and Declan felt the same way. They walked just as quickly as Harry did toward the elevators. Harry pressed the three on the panel, and the elevator took them quietly up to the third floor. None of them spoke during the walk to Hao's room. There was a very somber mood among them; it was so hard to believe that they had all been at Declan's birthday party less than seven hours ago with a happy and smiling Hao.

When they found his room, Harry knocked on the door. Mrs. Jones answered the door. She was a petite woman with large, warm eyes. She smiled right away when she saw the rest of the Good Mischief Team.

"Oh, good! I'm so glad you boys came. Hao will be so happy to see you!"

They filed in one by one with Harry leading. When Harry saw Hao on the bed, he felt a little relieved. Because he was in the hospital, Harry had been expecting something dramatic —like something out of a television forensics show. But instead, Hao was propped up in bed. A sophisticated-looking hanger kept his leg slightly elevated from the bed. With the exception of the cast, it looked almost comfortable.

"I'll give you boys some time to talk," Mrs. Jones said. "I could use some coffee anyway."

She took her exit as Harry, Declan, and Bailey all carefully crowded around the bed. The room was antiseptic and rather featureless. Everything in it looked very clean. On the front wall, a TV was mounted, showing a baseball game at low volume.

Harry wasn't sure how to react. His friend had just been hit by a car, but he looked to be in pretty good shape. Knowing Hao, he'd want them all to be laughing about it rather than worrying about him and being in sour moods.

"So what are you chumps waiting for?" Hao asked. He pulled a black magic marker out from under his sheets and handed it to Bailey. "Sign my cast!"

Bailey did just that, followed by Declan and then Harry. Harry wrote softly, not wanting to move the cast or Hao's leg.

"What's it feel like?" Bailey asked.

"It hurts; I won't lie about it," Hao said. "But right now, the itch from the cast is the worst thing."

"So if you're in a cast," Harry said, "why are they making you stay overnight?"

"They want to make sure it sets okay.

Tomorrow afternoon they'll do some kind of an x-ray to see if I need surgery. They don't think I will. They're just being safe."

"So what happened?" Declan said.

"Well, it was scary, but it was sort of cool, too," Hao said rather proudly. He spent the next five minutes describing the scene of the accident. He ended by telling them that he was going to have to get the back tire of his bike replaced, but other than that, his Lean, Mean, Speed Machine was going to be fine.

65

"So you were rushing to get to work, huh?" Harry asked.

"Yeah. I should have left the party earlier."

"Three jobs is too much," Harry said. "Are you sure you need them all?"

"Well, with a broken leg, I may not be able to work any of them for a few months," Hao said. "It's going to hurt the extra cash I had coming in to help mom, that's for sure."

The three of them looked awkwardly around the room for a while, clearly uncomfortable. Harry wished there was something he could do to make Hao feel better. He wondered if there was some sort of magic he could use to help the situation.

In their silence, Harry looked back up to the TV. The baseball game had gone to commercial. Harry's jaw nearly dropped to the floor when he saw two words stretched across the screen.

BIRTHDAY FANTASIES!

The screen was then filled with balloons and floating cupcakes. Upbeat, cheerful music blared. A single figure walked through all of it, coming to the center of the screen.

"Hey, guys," Harry said. "Look at this!"

On the screen, the figure emerged from the balloons. It was a face Harry had seen numerous times—a face that made him feel anxious and a little angry.

"Isn't that what's-his-face?" Bailey asked.

"Yeah," Harry said. "Titus's older brother."

Harry had more past experience with Marcus Kligore than he cared to think about. Much like the mayor, Harry and Marcus did not get along and, on more than one occasion, had crossed paths in dangerous ways.

The four boys watched the television with great interest. Harry wondered if anyone else was getting a sinking feeling in the pit of their stomach. Harry sure was.

67

On the screen, Marcus Kligore was dressed in an elaborate, purple suit. He wore dark sunglasses, had his hair slicked back, and, although Harry hated to admit it, looked pretty cool. Behind him, a few other characters appeared through the balloons. They were dressed as clowns, dancers, and sports figures. One of them was clearly Oink, dressed as a ballerina. Another was Ug, Oink's rat-like associate, in football garb. They were dancing around. They looked ridiculous. But the commercial seemed fun—another thing Harry hated to admit.

Marcus stared directly into the camera and gave a charming smile. Behind him, presents started to rain across the screen.

"Isn't it a shame that your birthday only comes around once a year?" Marcus asked the viewer. "Well, at Birthday Fantasies, we know how special a birthday can be. That's why we want to offer you the absolute best birthday experience money can buy! No matter what your interest is, Birthday Fantasies has a theme for you. From out-of-this-world decorations to delicious food of all kinds, we're your one-stop shop for all things birthday! From newborn kiddos to old geezers on their deathbed, Birthday Fantasies has something for everyone! So give us a call today at 666-4247! Make your birthday the most special day of the year!"

More balloons floated upward, revealing a black screen that ended the commercial with the phone number and the location . . . right

68

in the middle of Sleepy Hollow.

"They did your party, right?" Hao asked Declan.

"Yeah. Mom was still raving about how awesome of a job they did when I left the house. Now that I know this creep was behind it, I feel bad."

"Well, it was an awesome party," Bailey said.

69

They all looked at Harry, waiting for him to add something to the conversation. He was sure they were expecting him to gush about how much fun he had at the party—but they also knew about his storied past with Marcus Kligore. They also knew about his intense distrust of Mayor Kligore, his family, and anyone that worked for him.

"It was a good party," Harry said. "The best. But . . . well, look at Hao. He's got a broken leg because he was rushing to work to make money to be able to afford presents for all of these birthday parties everyone is having."

"And because he cut out in the middle of the road on the Lean, Mean, Speed Machine," Declan pointed out.

"True," Harry said. "But still, think about it. How many birthday parties have you guys been to already this year?"

They all thought about it for a moment.

"Sixteen," Declan said. "I think. It might be more. Maybe closer to twenty."

"Eighteen," Hao answered. "I keep count because of the cost of gifts."

"I don't even know," Bailey said. "I have a lot of cousins. Probably twenty or twenty-five."

"And I've been to fifteen," Harry said. "And I've done magic shows at another dozen or so."

"What's your point?" Declan asked.

"My point is that with gift giving, there's

a lot of money involved. We just don't always understand that because our parents pay for the gifts. And we put this pressure on them to get awesome gifts so we don't feel bad about giving a lame gift."

"He's got a point," Hao said, looking sadly at his leg. "There's way too much stressing out about birthdays. It kind of takes the fun out of them."

"And it looks like Marcus Kligore is trying to make bank off of it," Harry said.

His friends seemed to understand what he was getting at after mentioning the Kligores. The room seemed to grow a little colder as this settled over them.

"Is there anything we can do?" Bailey asked.

Again, all eyes were on Harry.

"I don't know," Harry said. "But if we're talking about some kind of birthday change, I think we need to start it. We need to be the examples."

The Good Mischief Team smiled at one another. Even Hao managed a smile from the hospital bed. On the TV, the baseball game was back on, and the four boys were able to relax and enjoy the last few minutes of their visit with Hao.

Still, in the back of his mind, Harry tried to think of how he and his friends could change the minds of so many kids. Getting gifts was great—but at what cost?

It was going to be a tough job, but if Harry had learned anything during his time as a kid magician, it was to never underestimate the influence of a few nagging and determined boys.

A Big, Fat,
Never-Ending Party

As it turned out, Harry wasn't able to get away from the news of Birthday Fantasies the following day. It was Monday, and everyone was over the moon about the few birthday parties that had occurred over the weekend. People were also talking about the commercial that the Good Mischief Team had seen on the TV in

Hao's hospital room.

Harry hadn't even been able to make it into homeroom before he heard people talking about the elaborate birthday parties they'd been to over the weekend. From what he could gather, one party had been football themed, and another had been outer space themed—complete with an anti-gravity chamber and authentic astronaut spacesuits.

74

People were also talking about Declan's party. One kid even had a black eye he'd accidentally received when a demonstration had gotten a little out of hand. All in all, the whole school was abuzz with the excitement of Birthday Fantasies. Harry also heard several kids talking about their upcoming birthdays and how they were going to get their parents to have Birthday Fantasies organize it.

One thing was for certain, whenever Mayor Kligore tried some new idea on the town, Sleepy Hollow Middle School seemed to latch on to it pretty quickly.

The only thing that cheered Harry up much that morning was when Mandy Mooney approached Harry just before lunch to ask about Hao. Mandy was a quiet girl for the most part, but the rest of the Good Mischief Team had always suspected she had a crush on Hao. The only one who *didn't* think so, of course, was Hao.

"How's Hao?" she asked, sliding up beside Harry as he made his way to the cafeteria.

75

"He's in good spirits," he answered. "They'll know if he needs surgery later today. If they decide there's no surgery needed, he should be back home tonight."

"That's great! Tell me; did he *really* get hit by a car?"

"Yeah. He was on his bike, though. The bike got hit. Not Hao."

"Well, that's a relief."

"Yeah."

"Did all of you guys go to any of the parties people keep talking about?" Mandy asked.

"Hao and I went to Declan's party. It was pretty cool but . . . well, a little much. It was crazy."

"That's what I hear. You know, I just don't get birthdays."

"What do you mean?" Harry asked.

"Well, when people go on and on about the gifts they get, they seem sort of snotty, you know? Like, after a while, no one wants to hear about your dumb gifts. It makes people sound selfish."

"I agree one hundred percent," Harry said.

"I don't like big parties anyway," Mandy said. "It's too busy. Too stressful."

Harry nodded in appreciation. It was good to know that he wasn't the only kid around that thought the idea of huge, elaborate, birthday parties and over-priced gifts were unnecessary. Maybe making a change within the town wouldn't be as impossible as he thought.

Now if he just knew how to start . . .

"Well, will you let Hao know that I asked about him?" Mandy asked, stopping by her locker.

"I sure will," Harry said.

91

As he headed down to the cafeteria, Harry passed by the local events bulletin board. Several kids were milling around it, laughing excitedly. Harry crowded in behind them, looking over shoulders to see what they were looking at.

In the center of the bulletin board, there was a huge flier. The all too familiar face of Marcus Kligore was front and center. Balloons and elegantly wrapped gifts surrounded him. Above it all, in huge letters, were two words that Harry was already tired

of hearing.

BIRTHDAY FANTASIES!

With a sigh, Harry left the crowd of fascinated kids and headed into the cafeteria even though he was suddenly not very hungry.

Mary Moon stirred a pot of boiling

macaroni. She looked at the small stack of mail on the kitchen counter. The usual junk mail and bills were there. Also, there were two other pieces of mail that had her really irked. One was addressed to Harry and the other to Honey. She had not opened them yet, but the decorative envelopes made it clear what they were.

More birthday invitations, she thought. *This is getting out of hand.*

Honey was still floating around on cloud nine over the invitation to Malory Marvel's party this weekend. And Mary Moon still needed to get a gift for that. If things kept up at this rate, she and John were going to have to sit down and figure out how to budget for all of the birthday gifts in their future.

She wondered when kids had become so entitled. At what point was it no longer deemed acceptable to give a nice, simple gift? Kids had gone from giving their friends ten-dollar gift cards to sixty-dollar video games and fancy dresses. The kids and the parents were equally to blame, really. Parents knew how much stress and money were involved in getting presents for other kids. But most parents seemed to forget about that fact when they were planning parties for their own kids. As for the kids, well, most of them just didn't care. When they started receiving gifts, manners and respect disappeared, and they cared only about themselves.

80

As she finished preparing dinner, she started to wonder how she could instill different values into her kids. She liked to think that Harry and Honey had good heads on their shoulders. And even though Honey had been stoked to receive Malory Marvel's invitation in the mail last week, she also knew the difference between being excited and being selfish.

"Dinner's almost ready," Mary Moon announced.

Within a minute or so, John Moon and

Honey were setting the table. Harvest pawed at his high chair and climbed into the seat on his own. Harry filled glasses of water and milk for their drinks.

The Moon family enjoyed dinner together. It was the one staple of family life that Mary Moon had long ago insisted that they would never skip unless it was absolutely necessary. With busy schedules filled with sports, school, and extracurricular activities, family dinners were of the utmost importance as far as she was concerned.

"I want to talk about something that might be a little upsetting to the two of you," Mary said, eyeing Harry and Honey.

"Great lead in, Mom," Honey said sarcastically.

"Look, both of you got mail today, and I am certain it's more birthday invitations. I really think this whole birthday thing has gotten to be too much, especially with this new company in town that hosts these extravagant parties."

"Birthday Fantasies," Harry said with a scowl.

"Yes, that's the one. Now, as you guys know, your dad and I have to pay for gifts for these parties."

"I can start paying for my own, Mom," Harry said. "I'm saving money from the magic shows."

"That's sweet, Harry. But I'm not going to make you do that. Now, what was I saying? We can't change the way other people do birthdays. Most kids these days live their lives as if it was nothing more than one big, fat, never-ending birthday party. Unfortunately, we can't change the way *everyone* thinks. But we can change the way *we* do parties."

"What do you mean, dear?" John asked.

Even little Harvest was looking in her direction, mac and cheese smeared on his face.

"I'm fine with you two having parties for your birthday," Mary said. "But we're done with receiving gifts. We need to give the kids and their parents a break."

"No gifts?" Honey asked.

"That's right."

Honey frowned, looked at her plate, but then nodded. "Okay."

83

"What did you have in mind?" Harry asked.

"I'm not sure, yet. We could tell the guests that instead of gifts, they can make a donation to a charity that you guys choose."

"That could be cool," Honey said.

"Yeah," Harry said. "Good thinking, Mom."

"Does anyone else have any ideas?" Mary asked. She was very pleased that her children had been so receptive to the idea. It warmed her heart and made her incredibly thankful for her family.

"We could try something new, too," Harry said. "Something cool that everyone else would catch on to. We could maybe even change the way people think of birthdays. We could do away with them altogether."

"Hey!" Honey said. "Let's not get carried away!"

"No, that's not what I mean," Harry said. "What I mean is a new way to celebrate. Like . . . I don't know. Maybe surprising people by celebrating their birthdays on a day that's not their birthday."

John Moon smiled widely from his spot at the head of the table. Mary Moon chuckled at the idea. Harvest slapped his hands into a heap of mac and cheese, sending it splattering to the floor.

"That's a wonderful idea," Mary said. "Now what would we call it?"

"A Not Your Birthday Birthday!" Harry exclaimed. He really felt like they had stumbled onto something special here.

"That's weird," Honey said.

"Yes, but it's different," John said. "It's unique."

Harry smiled, proud of himself. Yes, it was different, and it was unique. But more importantly, it gave kids and their parents an alternative to the selfish mindset behind Marcus Kligore's Birthday Fantasies.

Now, of course, the trick would be to get other people as excited about it as the Moon family was.

NOT YOUR BIRTHDAY BIRTHDAY

B y Tuesday, every student in Sleepy Hollow Middle School had heard about Birthday Fantasies. The silly commercial that Harry had seen in the hospital had significant airplay. Now, there were even more fliers up through the school and the town. Harry couldn't stand it—Marcus Kligore's face leered at him from every corner throughout the school.

Tuesday did offer up a bit of happiness, though. It came in the form of Bailey rushing toward him in the cafeteria at lunch.

"Did you hear the good news about Hao?" Bailey asked.

"No," Harry said. "What is it?"

88

"Well, they didn't have to do surgery on his leg, so he was able to come home last night. But the break itself was pretty bad, and he's going to have to miss school for a while."

"Have you talked to him?" Harry asked.

"No. My mom called to see if Mrs. Jones needed anything and got the update."

"How much school will he miss?"

"About two weeks," Bailey said.

"That stinks," Harry replied.

"Are you kidding?" Declan said, taking a seat and joining them. "I'd give anything to miss two weeks of school!"

"Would you willingly get your leg broken?" Bailey asked.

Declan considered it for a moment and then shook his head. Declan thought for a moment before he spoke further. "You know, guys—I snooped around a little after we visited Hao at the hospital."

"Snooped around where?" asked Harry.

"Well, I looked at my mom's checkbook," Declan said. His face flushed with embarrassment. "I saw how much my party cost. I know she wants to be a good mom, but it was insane."

"Really?" Bailey asked.

"Yeah. It was way out of line. And to see the check written to Birthday Fantasies made me feel sick."

Harry was about to respond but never got the chance. Out of nowhere, Clooney Mackay showed up. He didn't sit down at their table but sort of hovered around it. Clooney was in eighth grade but looked like a tenth grader. He'd been held back last year, and rumor had it that he had also been forced to repeat the fourth grade, making him look much older than most of the other middle school kids.

"Did you losers hear about the birthday party I'm having this weekend?" he beamed.

"No," Declan said. Harry and Bailey shook their heads.

"Of course not," Clooney said. "That's because you didn't get invited. Not even the magnificent Harry Moon and his baby magic show."

"Like we'd want to come to your party anyway," Bailey said.

"Oh, you would if you knew anything about it. We're having Birthday Fantasies put it on.

It's going to be race car themed. There's even going to be a go-cart track installed in the back yard."

"Really?" Bailey asked, apparently forgetting that they weren't supposed to be interested.

"Really," Clooney replied. "So what are you dorks doing this weekend?"

"We've got our own birthday party to go to," Harry said.

"Oh, I bet that'll be a lot of fun," Clooney said sarcastically. "Whatever party you go to, it won't be as good as mine. And I bet the birthday boy or girl won't get presents nearly as cool as mine!"

In that moment, Harry Moon felt something stir inside of him. It wasn't anger, but something very close to it. Usually, when he felt things like this, he bottled it up and kept it inside. He much preferred to keep a calm attitude, not letting emotions like sadness or anger show on the outside. But the last few days had been too much for him, and quite frankly, he was tired of keeping things bottled up.

Before he knew what he was doing, Harry got to his feet. When he did, he thought of Hao and what he must be feeling, shut-in at home with a busted leg. And how had his leg gotten that way? From rushing to his third job to make some extra money just so his mom wouldn't go broke having to buy endless birthday gifts for his friends.

"Oh, shove your race car birthday party," Harry said. "You know why your parents are throwing you a big birthday party? It's because you're spoiled, and the only way they know how to make you feel special is to spend money on your big, stupid party!"

Harry didn't realize that he had gotten loud until everyone in the cafeteria was looking in his direction. Rather than getting embarrassed, Harry decided that he should take advantage of the attention.

"What did you say to me?" Clooney said,

taking a step forward. He was getting red in the face, his eyes wide and angry.

Harry ignored him. He stepped up in his chair and then up onto the table. Standing over the eighty or so students in the cafeteria, he felt awkward, yet, at the same time, a little powerful. He didn't exactly enjoy the feeling, but he knew that if he didn't act now, he'd probably never find the courage to do it again.

"All of us, at some time or another, have rebelled against something that was expected of us, right?"

He got a few murmurs of agreement from the crowd.

"So why is it that birthday parties are any exception? Yeah, birthdays are great, and the gifts can be sweet, but enough is enough. The pressure on kids *and* parents is crazy! And now, not only are parents expected to shell out money to buy some crappy gift that's just going to be left in a closet, forgotten, within a week, but they're also now expected to pay extra money for these elaborate parties—parties with ninjas and race cars and astronauts."

Among more murmurs of agreement, Harry saw that Clooney Mackay had slunk back into the crowd, looking down at his feet, seemingly embarrassed. The attention from the crowd was making him dizzy, so Harry carried on before he had a chance to lose his nerve.

"Look, I like presents and parties just as much as the next guy. But this . . . this . . . *gluttony* on birthdays has got to stop! It's not fair to our parents, it's not fair to us most of the time, and it does nothing but prove a stereotype—the stereotype that kids today are spoiled and self-centered. Spending tons of cash on crazy birthday parties is the *last thing* we need. But right now, most of the kids in the school are going on and on about this new place, Birthday Fantasies. They are charging our parents outrageous amounts of money just to put on some over-the-top party for us. It's not right, it's not fair, and it's just a big rip-off, really. Are you with me?"

He got a few cheers from the crowd, but not many. He had one last push, one last idea to hopefully make this a moment of triumph rather than one of embarrassment.

"So why don't we make birthdays *ours* again? I propose that we start celebrating the Not Your

Birthday Birthday!"

A murmur of conversation rippled through the cafeteria. Near the back of the room, he saw Mrs. Knapp, the principal, storming forward with a very upset expression on her face. Harry guessed he had another ten seconds, at most, before he was asked to come down from the table.

"We don't even recognize someone's birthday," Harry explained, giving as much tenor to his voice as he could. "Instead, we surprise each other by celebrating somebody, anybody, on a completely random day. It'll always be a surprise, and it's more about celebrating the person rather than the day they were born. No expensive presents, no ridiculous, themed parties, and no pressure! Just fun, excitement, and friends . . . what a birthday *should* be!"

A loud cheer erupted through the cafeteria. He'd gotten most of them to listen, but a few seemed annoyed that he had interrupted their lunch.

"Mr. Moon," Mrs. Knapp said, now taking a very defiant stance at the end of the table. "You've had your time and your stage," she said. "Now, please do get down from the table."

Harry stood there for a moment, unmoving. He was waiting for a demand to head to the principal's office. When he realized it wasn't coming, he got down at once. His cheeks flushed red as he took his seat as the reality of what he had just done washed over him.

As the crowd started to break up, a few people came by to shake Harry's hand or clap him on the back. Harry had never even spoken to some of the kids. He thought he might have accomplished something— something that had not needed the aid of a wand, a magic hat, or even a magic Rabbit.

98

SHOWDOWN

The birthday invitation Harry had received earlier in the week—the invitation that had prompted the Not Your Birthday Birthday conversation at the Moon dinner table—had been for Mark Rutherford's party. He was turning fourteen and, as the invitation had explicitly made clear, the party was being thrown by Birthday Fantasies.

The party was scheduled for Saturday. Harry spent a great deal of time on Friday night trying to decide if he would go or not. He had gotten many thankful messages from students (and even a few faculty members) since giving his speech on Tuesday. He felt like attending a party being thrown by Birthday Fantasies might be hypocritical. But at the same time, he knew Mark Rutherford pretty well and did not want to seem rude by not going.

In the end, Harry decided to attend the party. He called Declan and Bailey to make sure they were going as well. On Saturday morning, Harry left the house and headed into town to buy a gift for the party. He purchased a gift from Chillie Willie's and made his first anti-birthday statement. He spent only half of what he would usually spend on a gift and then placed the other half into a collection jar that was raising money for sick children in a nearby town.

When he arrived at the party, he discovered that it was zombie themed. As much as Harry hated to admit it, the decorations and costumes were amazing. The performers from Birthday

Fantasies looked far too real—so much so that a few kids in attendance wouldn't go within several feet of them. Some had eyes dangling out of their sockets while others had gaping holes in their stomachs with their insides falling out. As far as Harry was concerned, it all looked a little too real.

He also couldn't help but wonder if Oink was hiding under any of those disguises. Or maybe Marcus was hiding under one. Harry doubted this, though. Rumor had it that Marcus Kligore was a lazy, spoiled brat. If he could be sitting in an office with his feet propped up, he'd surely not be attending a fourteen-year-old's party dressed as one of the undead.

Inside, the house was decorated with blood splatters everywhere. A few very life-like mannequins were on the floor missing various limbs. Harry took it all in as he looked for Declan and Bailey. He found them in the dining area where a large table had been set out with party snacks: grapes that looked like eyeballs, Jell-O that looked like squished brains, mini-hotdogs that resembled decapitated fingers, and some sort of red drink that looked far too much like actual blood for Harry's liking.

"So, this is interesting," Harry said.

"It's creepy is what it is," Bailey said.

"I think it's awesome," Declan said. "If not a little . . . weird."

The three of them ventured through the party. Even though they were at a Birthday Fantasies birthday party, Harry still got the occasional high five in regards to his infamous speech in the cafeteria.

Elsewhere in Mark Rutherford's house, they found several boys playing a very loud game called Zombie Apocalypse. Harry stayed away, preferring the back of the room where Declan and Bailey kept him company.

As they stood there and watched the party, it took Harry no time to find a very particular zombie within the crowd that was wearing a fairly obvious disguise. He narrowed his eyes at the performer, recognizing Oink right away. He was parading around with his arms outstretched, and his face was made up to look as if his skin was peeled back to reveal his skull.

Seeing Oink, Harry felt the same stirring of anger that he had felt in the cafeteria and worried that he'd do something else foolish.

Stay calm, Harry, he told himself. *Stay calm.*

"I'll be right back," Harry said. "I need some water."

He left his friends and headed back upstairs where there were fewer zombies to sidestep. He beelined to the snack table where he grabbed a bottle of water from the cooler and then wandered through the house among zombies and birthday party attendees in search of the restroom. He found the restroom and closed himself in it for a while. He splashed water onto his face over the sink hoping it would relax him.

When he patted his face dry, he found that he was no longer alone in the restroom. Rabbit was sitting in the tub, his paws on the edge, peering out at him.

"You seem troubled, Harry," Rabbit said simply.

"I am," Harry said. "This whole Birthday Fantasies thing . . . it makes me angry. And I don't like being angry."

"I don't think anyone likes to be angry," Rabbit said. "But you know, it's okay to feel that way from time to time."

"It is?"

"Yes, indeed. The trick, though, is to make sure you don't spoil whatever justice you have in mind *with* your anger. Do you understand?"

"Sort of," he said.

"Well, when you see others being mistreated —when you see injustice and evil being done while the guilty not only get away with it but don't care that they are doing wrong—that's an anger that is almost noble. Seeing those unjust things makes you want to act. They make you want to stand up for the people being mistreated. Is that what you're feeling?"

"I think so," Harry said.

Rabbit hopped out of the tub and walked up close to Harry. "There's something else, isn't there?" Rabbit asked.

"Yes. I think . . . well, I think I have to do something to put a stop to all of this."

"Like your speech in the lunchroom?" Rabbit asked. "That would be nice. You *are* quite the orator."

"Rabbit, is it okay for me to act on this anger?"

Rabbit seemed to consider this for a moment. "There is a very fine line between justice and revenge, and if you are representing the Good Magic, you have to know that line well. Do you understand?"

"Justice over vengeance?"

"Good. Now, do you have your wand on you?"

"Yes," Harry said, his hand going to his hip where he usually kept his wand hidden in the waist of his pants whenever he knew the potential for trouble was at hand. "Why do you ask?"

Rabbit gave a knowing little grin. He looked at the bathroom door and then shrugged. "You never know when you might need it. Go in peace, Harry. Or, if you must, in justice."

Harry left the restroom and instantly found the hallway blocked. Marcus Kligore was standing in front of him.

He was dressed in zombie attire—a ripped shirt with fake blood and stained pants. He wore zombie makeup, but Harry thought the

true nature of Marcus shined through even worse than the walking dead.

"There's the little speech writer," Marcus said. "Were you in there talking to yourself or something?"

Not wanting to bother trying to explain himself, Harry ignored him completely. "Excuse me," Harry said. He walked by Marcus. As he passed, Harry was sure Marcus would slug him, but he didn't.

"From what I hear, no one can shut you up," said Marcus. "That is when you're standing on a lunch table in front of a bunch of loser eighth graders. But now that I'm here, what do you have to say about my company now?"

Harry didn't know if it was his feeling of being provoked by injustice or if he was just downright mad, but *something* caused him to stop and turn around. He thought of Rabbit asking if he had his wand. Had Rabbit sensed that trouble was coming? Probably.

Harry did not back down. He thought of the stories he'd heard of David and Goliath. He sort of wished he had a sling and a rock.

"What do I have to say about your company?" Harry asked, summoning all of his courage. "I think it's a pathetic attempt to squeeze every drop of money possible from the people in this town just so they can give their kids a birthday party. I think you're playing on a kid's need to compete and try to be better and—"

108

"This is boring me already," Marcus said. "Oink, would you please?"

Harry turned around and saw Oink standing behind him, holding the bowl of eyeball grapes in his hands. Oink smiled at Harry and then dumped the entire bowl on Harry's head. It was cold and slimy and, more than anything, embarrassing.

Marcus leaned down to Harry and grinned. "That looks gross. You just remember this the next time you bad-mouth Birthday Fantasies."

Harry defiantly swiped the grapes from his head onto Marcus's shirt. They splattered into the carpet, too. The place was really becoming a mess.

"Walk away, Harry Moon," Marcus said. He said it softly but with spite and hatred. "Go now before I get really mad."

Harry was fuming. His heart was pounding, and he was shaking with rage. Still, he knew that he had to be the bigger man in this situation. He could not let a few slimy grapes make him act in a way that was unbecoming.

Harry looked down at the floor, turned, and shouldered past Oink. He was mortified to see that several of the partygoers had gathered in the hall. They had seen the whole thing. Some were snickering and pointing. He saw Declan and Bailey in the mix, slowly coming through the crowd to join him in leaving.

Harry was headed for the door when Marcus started to applaud. "That's right boys and girls, that's your middle school magician,

Harry Moon! Thwarted by grapes and unable to harness the Good Magic to keep himself from getting dirty. Let's give him a round of applause and—"

ABRACADABRA*!*

The word was out of Harry's mouth before he knew it.

At the same time, his hand went to his waist and pulled out his wand as if it were a light saber. Following the magic word, the plate of Jell-O came rocketing out of the dining room and down the hall. It flew with incredible speed, a yellow and green blur of gelatin, and came to a horrific, splattering stop on Marcus's face.

Harry stood his ground, watching as the plate slid to the floor. When it dropped, Marcus's Jell-O covered face leered at him.

"You're going to regret that!" Oink said, barreling forward in defense of Marcus.

Harry gave a quick flick of his wrist and the grapes from his head were suddenly flying at Oink. They pelted his face in wet squirts. Two of them landed directly in his eyes, causing him to stumble blindly forward. He ping-ponged off the walls, making little grunting noises. As he neared the dining room, Declan stuck out his foot.

"Whoops," Declan said with a laugh.

Oink stumbled and went to the floor. Harry watched it all with a smile on his face. He then turned to look back at Marcus . . . and was about one second too late to defend himself.

The punch was a little low, maybe because of the Jell-O in Marcus's eyes, so it missed Harry's jaw by about three inches. Still, Marcus's fist landed squarely on Harry's chest. The pain was terrible and sent Harry stumbling backward.

Before Harry was able to regain his footing, Marcus advanced. Another punch sailed forward. This one landed true, hitting Harry in the right eye. He went spiraling to the ground, unable to believe how badly it hurt. Marcus marched toward Harry.

Extending his wand, Harry pointed to the first place he could find, and yelled *"ABRACADABRA!"*

The shoelaces on Marcus's boots whipped outwards, untying themselves and then looping into a knot, holding the shoes together. Marcus tried to take a step forward before he realized what had happened. Slowly, he started to lose his balance.

Harry looked Marcus directly in the eyes and raised his wand. He then recited a series of words that came to him from some unknown place within his head.

"His dumb zombie lurch!
His cold Jell-O eyes!
Let's all give Marcus
A big birthday surprise!"

112

Again, a plate came floating out of the dining room. Harry guided it with his wand, bringing the plate, and the large birthday cake that sat on it, closer to Harry. In front of him, Marcus, only seconds from falling, teetered in front of Harry..

Harry carefully aimed his wand, resting the cake at his feet. It was a three-tier cake with a very realistic zombie face drawn out in icing, no doubt an addition added on by Birthday Fantasies.

There were tons of cream and frosting. It

looked delicious.

It was a shame it was about to go to waste.

"You're making the biggest mistake of your life," Marcus said.

Harry did not reply. He simply stepped back and watched Marcus fall face-first into the cake. The sound made a delicious *splat* noise. Immediately, everyone in the party roared with laughter and applause.

For the second time that week, Harry was greeted with pats on the backs and high fives. In the midst of the revelry, Marcus Kligore started to move on the floor. Oink was also starting to get to his wobbly feet.

"Yeah, yeah," Declan said. "That was awesome, Harry. Now let's get out of here before we're killed."

Together, the three members of the Good Mischief Team hauled tail out of the front door with the other party members cheering from behind. Harry's chest was hurting, and he could already feel his eye starting to swell shut.

Still, before they even reached the end of the block, they were laughing harder than they had laughed in a very long time.

116

GROUNDED

The first thing Mary Moon did when Harry arrived home from Mark Rutherford's party was rush to him and sweep him into her arms. By then, his right eye had swollen almost completely shut, and the bruise reached down to his cheek. When she hugged him and Harry grimaced, she also discovered the bruise on his chest.

When he refused to tell her what had happened, the second thing Mary Moon did was grow suspicious. Harry did not want her to know that Marcus Kligore had done these things to him. The thought of his mother getting mixed up with the mayor and his family was terrifying, and Harry would simply not have it.

118

However, when Gabrielle Rutherford, Mark's mother, called later to tell Mary that her son had started a fight at her home that had made a terrible mess, things got worse. When he still would not tell his mother the whole story, she grounded him. She also informed him that they would be visiting the doctor to make sure there was no real harm

So, on Sunday, they went to the ER just to be certain there was no damage to Harry's eye. When he was given the all clear, they headed back home where Mary and John Moon again tried to get Harry to share the entire story of what had happened. Harry could not find a way to talk about it.

Sunday was very tense around the Moon household as Harry was tasked with keeping ice on his eye every half an hour. He also had to take medicine to help the pain subside and the swelling go down. And the entire time, he tried avoiding his parents at all costs. The ER doctor suggested he take at least one day off from school to allow the swelling to properly go down. He was proud of standing up to Marcus at the party, but it was starting to cause a lot of problems.

As Harry prepared to settle down for sleep, there was a knock at his door.

"Who is it?" he asked.

Mary Moon cracked the door open and peeked inside. "Just me," she said.

"Come in," Harry said.

His mother sat down on the end of his bed and gave him a weary smile. "I can't say that I like the look of a rough and rugged Harry Moon. Bruises don't suit you."

"Do they suit anyone?" Harry asked.

"Your father got into a fight when we were dating. He had a pretty bad scratch and bruise on the side of his face for a while. It was sort of charming—endearing in a way. But you, no, you're too handsome for black eyes."

120 Harry smiled, looking away. He hated to keep things from his parents, and the kindness of his mother was making this far too difficult.

"I'm not going to ask you about what happened at the party anymore," she said. "If you feel strongly about this, I know there has to be a good reason for the secrecy. Would that be correct?"

"That's right," Harry said.

"But the question I have for you is this: was the reason worth the black eye?"

Harry had thought about this most of the day. And every single time he recalled the memory of Marcus Kligore falling to the floor face-first into a cake, he decided that it had been *totally* worth it.

"Yes, I think so."

"Are you . . . well, are you in any trouble?" she asked.

"I don't know," he answered honestly. He hadn't dared to dwell too much on what sort of revenge Marcus would be looking for. He'd have to grow eyes in the back of his head to make sure he wasn't attacked. The more he thought about it, the more frightened he became.

"But you'd tell your father and me if you needed help with something, right?" Mary asked.

"Absolutely."

Mary Moon leaned over and kissed Harry

on the forehead. "That really is a nasty shiner you got there," she said. "Good night."

"Good night, Mom."

Mary left him alone, and he turned out the lights and went to bed. He thought of Marcus Kligore splatting into a cake and fell asleep peacefully with a smile on his bruised face.

Harry had never stayed at home without being sick. Mrs. Wilcox was also at the Moon home, taking care of Harvest. The morning dragged by very slowly as he was propped up on the couch, ice pack on his eye, reading a book by Elvis Gold, his favorite illusionist.

By the time lunch came around, Harry didn't think the day would ever end. He had a lot to think about, but that just seemed to make the day stretch out even longer. He thought about how he'd be received back at school with his black eye. He thought about what sort of horrible payback Marcus was surely waiting to inflict

upon him. He thought about Hao and wondered how he managed to make use of these days stuck at home.

Harry straightened up his room, did the dishes, made towers with Harvest and his building blocks, and finished off the Elvis Gold book.

He was thinking of starting another book when he caught sight of something out of the living room window. Someone was walking around out there—two people, then three.

It looked like they were trying to be very secretive about something.

Alarmed, Harry went to the window and looked out. When he did, someone jumped up at the window. Harry let out a shout of surprise and nearly fell on his butt. The face in the window smiled at him, and Harry was puzzled to see that it was Bailey.

Harry looked at the living room clock and saw that it was 3:30; school had let out half an hour ago. He then looked back to the yard and saw several other kids. He saw Declan, Mark Rutherford, Mandy Mooney, and a dozen other kids. Some of them were carrying balloons. Tom Bowlinger was even out there with the trumpet he was always tooting around the band room at school. Harry listened closely and was pretty sure he was playing (or, more accurately, *trying* to play) "Happy Birth-day."

Bailey rapped at the glass. "Come on out!"

"I can't leave the house! I'm already in

enough trouble!"

"Well, then sit back and enjoy! And . . . *happy birthday!*"

"Um, Bailey," Harry said through the window. "It's not my birthday."

"You're right. It's not! It's your Not Your Birthday Birthday!"

At that exact moment, two kids he knew from school came running across the lawn with a banner. It was obvious that the banner had been thrown together quickly, but that was fine with Harry. It was one of the friendliest gestures he'd ever seen.

The banner read *HAPPY NOT YOUR BIRTHDAY BIRTHDAY, HARRY!*

Several others were wearing party hats and blowing kazoos. Declan was among this group, blowing so hard on the kazoo that his face was turning red. Meanwhile, Tom Bowlinger kept tooting on his horn. He really wasn't very good with the instrument, but at that moment, it was beautiful music to Harry. As he watched his friends dance around his yard with balloons and banners, a sudden realization swept over Harry.

His idea had taken off. This was the first Not Your Birthday Birthday party, and from what he could tell, the kids out there on his lawn were having a blast.

Harry smiled and felt what his mother called "happy tears" coming to the corners of his eyes. It stung his busted eye a bit, but he barely noticed. He continued to watch his friends parade across the lawn, waving at him and laughing. Harry was pretty sure he had never been so happy in all of his life.

"It's very special, isn't it?" someone asked from behind him.

Harry turned around and saw Rabbit hopping to the window with a grin on his face. "What's special?" Harry asked.

"Friendship," Rabbit said.

"Yes, it is."

"You've got some great friends, Harry. They understand the sacrifice you made to make a stand for something they were too afraid to speak out about. One day, when your friends need something from you, remember this moment."

"Oh, that won't be a problem," Harry said. 127

He stood by the window with Rabbit, watching the party. He scratched Rabbit gently between the ears and couldn't stop smiling.

Mary Moon had been thinking of a way to discipline Harry all the way home. She was pretty sure she'd get home at least ten minutes before Honey got off of the bus. She'd use that ten minutes to have a hard heart-to-heart with Harry, and they'd figure out how to handle his incident at Mark

Rutherford's party. It would be a tough conversation but—

Mary's thoughts derailed as she reached her driveway. She saw the absolute craziness on her front lawn and, for a moment, was quite upset. But then she saw the party hats, heard the terrible trumpet music, and saw the banner being swept back and forth across the yard. She observed Harry looking out the window and smiling.

In the back of her head, she heard something that Samson had once told her long ago. Samson popped into her head from time to time, usually when Harry seemed to be struggling. What he had told her was: *You can't write the stories for your children; you can only help them turn the pages.*

One such page had been turned at the dinner table a few nights ago. Before Harry's black eye and his secrecy, there had been his passion to do something about the gluttony surrounding birthdays. Now, seeing the Not Your Birthday Birthday party in her front yard, she was pretty certain that whatever had happened at the Rutherford party had been about Harry making a stand.

She slowly rolled her car into the driveway. Bailey and a few other kids she didn't know very well waved at her. When she stepped out of the car, she was handed a kazoo, a party hat, and a cupcake. She took them all with a confused smile on her face. But when Tom Bowlinger came up behind her tooting his trumpet and dancing, Mary Moon started to move her feet.

Before long, she was dancing. She was dancing, blowing her kazoo, and staring into the window at her son.

After a while, she beckoned him outside. He came rushing out of the door within seconds and came directly to her. He hooked his arm through hers and looked up at her with happy tears in his eyes.

"I'm sorry, Mom," he said. "I'm sorry for not telling you everything. But, I have to handle this on my own for now."

"I know," she said, nodding and feeling her own happy tears stinging her eyes. "But let's not worry about that. For now, Happy Not Your Birthday Birthday, Harry."

130

CUPCAKES

As if receiving his own Not Your Birthday Birthday party wasn't great enough, Harry was fortunate enough to see five different Not Your Birthday Birthday parties spontaneously break out at school. They were taking place in the halls, in the cafeteria, and, much to Mrs. Knapp's disappointment, in the classrooms.

More than that, word of Harry's bravery at the Rutherford birthday party was spreading through school. He was getting so many high fives that his hand started to sting halfway through the week. He also noticed that the huge flier for Birthday Fantasies on the bulletin board going into the cafeteria had been defaced. Marcus Kligore now wore a pair of Sharpie glasses, had crazy hair, and a long tongue panting out like a dog. Someone had also added a word balloon to the side that said, "No more cake, please! Harry Moon RULZ!"

On Thursday afternoon, as Harry was headed for his last class of the day, he passed Titus Kligore in the hallway. Titus stopped and stared Harry down. The stare was filled with so much contempt that Harry could feel it stinging him. He had made so much progress with Titus. But it was clear that Marcus, the older brother, must have made him bitter once again.

While the congrats and the growing popularity of the Not Your Birthday Birthday were great, there was one thing in particular that made Harry's week even better. News had gotten out through the middle school grapevine that Hao was returning to school earlier than expected. He was coming on

Friday, escorted by his mother, to meet with teachers and to get assignments so he didn't fall too far behind.

Harry, Bailey, and Declan got to school early, all driven by Mary Moon who was in on their plan. When they arrived, Harry was not all that surprised to find that Mandy Mooney was also there to take part. She was holding a plate of cupcakes and looked a little embarrassed.

133

"Thanks for coming," Harry told her.

"Of course."

"Hao will really appreciate it."

Mandy said nothing. She sort of giggled and just looked at the floor. The four of them ran to the library and started setting up. Harry knew that Hao was supposed to meet Mrs. Knapp in the library to go over the week's missed assignments. Hao had given Harry the details on the phone last night when he mentioned the news that he was coming back to school early.

The four of them worked quickly, putting up banners and dishing out party hats to anyone that wanted to attend Hao's Not Your Birthday Birthday party. Just as Harry was finishing with the banner, tying it to the top of a bookcase (and wishing he could wield his wand in school to help), Mark Rutherford came rushing into the library.

134

"He's coming down the hall," Mark said. "We've got about twenty seconds!"

Everyone got quiet and hunkered down behind tables and bookcases. When the door opened several seconds later, and the sound of clicking crutches could be heard, they all got to their feet and belted out a very loud, "SURPRISE!"

Harry watched as Hao's face went through about a million expressions at once. He reeled back on his crutches, his blue cast wobbling. If his mother had not been standing behind him to catch him, he might have fallen on his tail. But in the end, Hao grinned widely as he crutched his way into the library.

135

"What is *this?*" he asked.

"It's your Not Your Birthday Birthday party," Harry explained.

"Just a warm welcome back to school," Declan said.

"Uh, yeah," Mandy added, her eyes still glued nervously to the floor.

Several kids came by to sign Hao's cast. A party hat was placed on his head as he ate a cupcake. The good times carried on for several minutes until Mrs. Knapp came in. She looked around for a moment and did a poor job of hiding her smile. She let it linger on her face for a while before she turned serious.

"Yes, yes, it is great to have Hao back," she said, "but we have business to attend to. So please, children, kindly make your way to class."

The children slowly obeyed, taking turns shaking hands with Hao or giving him high fives as they made their exit. As Harry went by, Hao grabbed his hand to make him stop.

"Thanks for this, Harry," Hao said. "I heard about everything that happened. This really means a lot."

"No problem. I'm just glad to have the whole Good Mischief Team back together."

"Me, too," Hao said.

Harry took his leave and left Hao to his mother and Mrs. Knapp. On his way to homeroom, Mandy Mooney stopped him. She still looked embarrassed but also a little nervous.

"Hey, Harry?" she said.

"Yeah?"

"Well, I haven't told anyone . . . but my birthday is today. I really want to get on board with the whole Not Your Birthday Birthday thing, but my mother already invited family and friends to my party tomorrow."

"Is it a Birthday Fantasies party?" Harry asked.

"Oh, goodness no," Mandy said. "And that's just the thing, I was wondering if you would come and do a magic show? And you know . . . maybe invite Hao."

"Of course," Harry said. "I'd love to. And I'm sure Hao would, too."

"Great," Mandy said, finally looking away from the floor. "I'll see you then!"

Smiling, Harry watched Mandy go. He made his way to homeroom, and as he did, he saw Titus Kligore staring at him from across the hall. Harry felt the hatred seeping off of Titus again, but this time he did not let it bother him. Instead, he gave Titus a bright smile and continued on his way. He would work on his friendship with Titus another day.

PARTY CRASHERS

Mandy Mooney's party was a small affair. There were maybe a dozen kids from school, including Hao. He looked uncomfortable in the cast but was glad to be out around his friends. Harry was pleased to see that Hao spent a great deal of time speaking with Mandy. The rest of the party consisted of Mandy's family, including several cousins all under ten years of age. They watched Harry with fascination as he set up for his magic show.

Harry geared most of the tricks toward the younger kids. He did some simple card tricks, making one disappear and then reappear in a kid's pocket. He made broken glasses mend themselves, used his wand to make one child's head float from one set of shoulders to another's. He tried out a new trick where he made a quarter pass through a mirror. They were all fairly simple tricks, but the kids loved it. As usual, he ended his show by pulling Rabbit out of his hat.

"Now," Harry said, waving his wand at Rabbit, "speak like a dog."

Rabbit seemed to roll his eyes and said, "Woof!"

"Now, a frog!"

Rabbit audibly sighed and then said, "Ribbit."

With that, Rabbit hopped back into Harry's hat. Harry then held the hat upside down to reveal that Rabbit was not inside; he had disappeared.

The audience went crazy. Even the rest of the Good Mischief Team, who had seen the trick countless times, were on their feet to applaud.

Harry took a few bows and then announced that cookies and cake were being served in the kitchen. As the crowd broke up and headed that way, Harry started to clean up his small stage and equipment.

As he was finishing up, a voice spoke up from behind him. It sent a cold chill down his spine, forcing him to turn around.

"There's the stupid, little magician," the voice said.

Harry found himself face-to-face with Marcus Kligore. Oink and Ug stood by his side. All three looked at Harry with great malice.

"What are you doing here?" Harry demanded.

"Crashing this lame party," Marcus said. "I told you that you'd regret what you did to me last weekend. I'm *still* blowing icing out of my nose because of your little trick. By the way, that black eye looked awesome on you. I think maybe you need another one to match it."

Harry readied his wand and took a step forward.

"Ug, if you please," Marcus said.

Ug's tail whipped up with blinding speed. It knocked the wand from Harry's hand, sending it across the room. The three villains instantly started advancing toward Harry. Harry knew that he had no way out. He was just going to have to take this pounding and hope it wasn't so bad that he ended up on crutches like Hao.

"My dad has always told me what a nuisance you are," Marcus said as he closed in. "Always getting in his way, meddling where you don't belong. That ends now. I can't wait to tell him that I finally took care of that little pipsqueak Harry Moon."

With a killer's grin, Marcus came even closer. He started making fists out of his hands. All Harry could do was back slowly away and hope that he didn't start crying or yelling.

Marcus brought his arm back to throw his first punch. Harry attempted to stand his ground, wanting to seem brave, wanting to—

143

Suddenly, something green and wet splashed against Marcus's leg. Confused, it took Harry a while to figure out what had happened. When Marcus turned around to look behind him, it all became clear, though.

Eleven eighth-graders stood on the other side of the room. All but one of them held a cup of punch. Hao looked at his empty hand with fake confusion and said, "Whoops. Sorry. It must have slipped right out of my hand. These crutches make me clumsy."

"Oh, you think that's *funny* you little creep?" Marcus asked. Furious now, he ignored Harry for the moment and advanced toward Hao. When he did, all eleven kids revealed the cupcakes they had been hiding behind their backs.

Without warning, half of them came sailing across the room. Most struck Marcus, but a few also struck Oink and Ug. Just as the cupcakes had been launched, a few more cups of punch came sloshing forward. One of the plastic cups struck Ug directly between the eyes. He let out a squeal and took a hasty retreat, speeding through the crowd of eighth graders in fear and embarrassment with his twisty tail trailing behind him.

In the midst of the confusion, Harry dashed to the right and retrieved his wand. As his hand fell on it, Marcus came rushing forward with his fist drawn back. He looked hilarious covered in icing once again, but it made that huge, chiseled fist look no less threatening.

When he was two steps away from Harry,

Mandy Mooney rolled a cupcake across the floor as if she were bowling. Her aim was perfect. It landed under Marcus's foot. It was a big, gooey cupcake, and when his foot landed on it, he lost his footing. Marcus went sailing upward as his feet went out from under him. He was suspended in the air for a split second and then came down hard on the floor. The entire house seemed to shake when he hit.

Harry turned his wand to Oink. Oink tried his best to look mean and menacing, but he was visibly shaking. Harry looked back to the eighth graders and said, "You guys like bacon?"

Oink's eyes got huge, and like Ug before him, he turned and ran.

Slowly, the eighth graders started circling Marcus Kligore. He was getting to his feet slowly, grimacing from the pain of having just slammed into the floor. He looked all around at the defiant faces, but his eyes eventually locked on Harry's.

"This is far from over," Marcus said. "In fact, if you're half the magician you think you are, you'd come outside and settle this man-to-man."

Harry nodded. "We can do that," he said. "But don't forget how things ended the last time you tried to get the best of me."

Marcus thought about this and shook his head. "Some other time, Moon Man. You're as good as dead. And all of you—" he said, pointing to the gathered kids.

He never got to finish, though. Bailey, Declan, and Hao were now holding what was intended to be Mandy Mooney's birthday cake.

"Make a wish," Declan said as they threw it forward.

The sound of the cake smashing into Marcus's face was one of the funniest noises Harry had ever heard. It had been so unexpected that Marcus went to the floor again. This time, though, he knew that he had no chance. He

started scrambling backward toward the Moody's front door. When he finally made it out, not a single inch of his face was visible. It was all covered in cupcake and birthday cake icing.

"With all that cake on his face," Bailey said, "it looks like today was Marcus's Not Your Birthday Birthday!"

The kids erupted in laughter while Harry looked out of the door and watched Marcus scramble, defeated, behind Ug and Oink. While it was a glorious sight to behold, Harry had seen a Kligore retreat before and assumed they were defeated, only to have them reappear more determined than ever.

But for now, he was not going to let that bother him. The twelve eighth-graders in attendance had stood up for something today. More than that, they had taken Harry's side and potentially saved him from a beating. That and the awesome Not Your Birthday Birthday party he'd been thrown earlier in the week made him feel very grateful.

Harry turned away from the door as Marcus and his minions disappeared around the block. He headed back to the party and joined his friends, who were already starting to clean up the mess that had sent Marcus Kligore packing.

THE FAMILY BUSINESS

When Marcus walked into the cellar of his father's mansion at Folly Farm that night, he still had cupcake frosting in his ears, sticky punch in his hair, and birthday cake in his nose. He was embarrassed, defeated, and quite funny looking. Still, as he took the elevator down 666 stories for a briefing on his progress to date, he didn't bother wiping any of it away. Keeping it there fueled his anger—it made him feel like nothing could stop him, and anything that *tried* to stop him would be obliterated. He also knew the job had to be finished.

150

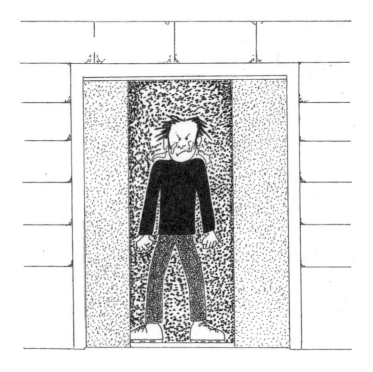

The elevator came to a stop two minutes later. When the old door slid open on its rusty hinges, the world was much darker and way hotter than it had been topside. He marched toward the Underground Grotto with his anger still pushing him along, the frosting like war paint on his face. When he took his place, he heard a wicked, feminine laugh from the other end of the large table.

It was Lady Dra Dra. She was laughing at him, her gorgeous eyes boring into him like a drill. In fact, everyone was present that had been in attendance when Birthday Fantasies had been created and handed over to Marcus—The Quiet Ones, Oink, the mayor. Like Marcus, Oink also showed signs of his defeat, with frosting still smeared on his head. His head was lowered, not wanting to be embarrassed in the presence of The Quiet Ones, sitting across from him, or the man at the head of the table—Mayor Kligore.

151

"Well, you look ridiculous," Mayor Kligore said. "What do you have to say for yourself?"

"It was that meddling little Harry Moon," Marcus said through clenched teeth. "I don't know how it happened, but he got the best of me. He got the eighth graders on his side.

It was a massacre."

"A cupcake massacre?" Lady Dra Dra asked humorously from the end of the table.

"Oh, I'm so glad you think it's funny," Marcus spat.

"Watch your tone, son," Mayor Kligore said. "Keep in mind who you're talking to. And," he said, gesturing to The Quiet Ones, "who's watching you."

Marcus took a moment to compose himself before he spoke again. "I'm sorry, Dad. I'm sorry, Lady Dra Dra. I've failed, and I'm sorry."

"Well," Lady Dra Dra said. "As terrible as the incident this afternoon was, I'm happy to report that things aren't nearly as bad as you think they are. Yes, you were bested by a group of eighth graders, and it's very likely that we will never get any business from that age group, but have you seen the Birthday Fantasies calendar?"

"Not since last weekend," Marcus said.

"You'll learn more about the business end of things as you grow," the mayor said. "Your time with the company is far from over."

"You mean you're going to keep me around?" Marcus asked.

"Indeed we are," Lady Dra Dra said. "Despite the eighth-grade mishap, business is booming. We have thirty-two parties booked through the next three months alone. Graduation parties, birthday parties, retirement parties. There's no end to it. And one of the pieces of feedback we continuously get from young girls and, in some cases, older ladies, is they love the handsome young man that leads it all. And your endless need to have fun makes you the perfect candidate to throw amazing parties."

Marcus grinned. Already, the defeat from earlier in the day was starting to sting less. "So the business is still doing well?"

"Very well. Birthday Fantasies is an enormous

hit with the high school and the nearby colleges. We're growing bigger and bigger with each party we throw. You're doing well, Marcus. Don't let this one mishap detour you."

"I won't."

One of The Quiet Ones made a faint whispering noise. Its robes seemed to shimmer as it spoke.

"What did it say?" Mayor Kligore asked.

"It said that this Harry Moon problem cannot get out of hand," Lady Dra Dra said. "Mr. Zebub can only tolerate so much failure, especially from such a small foe."

"Look," Marcus said. "I hate admitting it . . . but that kid scares me. There's something about him . . ."

"I know the feeling," the mayor said.

"That does not matter," Lady Dra Dra said. "The next time he interferes with our business, we may have to take . . . *extreme* measures."

This thought settled over the Underground Grotto as the infinite fire in the fireplace crackled and roared. Marcus plucked a chunk of frosting from his hair and flicked it into the fire. The hissing noise it made was satisfying, and it helped him to calm down. Better yet, it helped him to wonder what Harry Moon's body might sound like in that fire.

And just like that, Marcus Kligore was in a much better mood. He felt like he could rule Birthday Fantasies until it was a massive success that helped keep *We Drive By Night* afloat.

155

"You're doing well, son," Mayor Kligore said. "I'm proud of you."

Marcus smiled again. Yes, he was going to be just fine. And after he was done ruling Birthday Fantasies, why not all of New England?

Mary Moon was sitting in her glider on the porch, looking out into the back yard. The Good Mischief Team was out there, playing a variation of tag. She wasn't quite sure how the rules worked, but she thought Hao, still very immobile due to the crutches, was serving as base.

She watched Harry closely, finding it hard to believe that he was only thirteen. Sometimes the things he endured and thought of made her feel like he was much older. She knew that her son was special in ways that she would never understand. She'd know that even if she had not been approached by Samson before Harry had even been born.

She had caught bits and pieces about what had happened at Mandy Mooney's party through other parents. She knew that Marcus Kligore had tried crashing the party and then had his butt handed to him by Harry and a dozen or so eighth graders. From that, she assumed the black eye had come from Marcus at another party.

Rather than going to Marcus's father about the confrontation, Mary had left it alone. Again, she referred back to what Samson had told her about Harry needing to write his own story.

Whatever it was about Harry that was special, she knew that it went beyond her understanding. But whatever it was, it was good, and it was safe, and she knew it would keep Harry safe from harm.

171

She was beyond proud of him and, quite frankly, felt that he was growing up too fast.

She was pulled from her loving thoughts by a text message. She checked it and saw that it was the mother of one of Honey's friends. They were in the process of planning Honey's Not Your Birthday Birthday party. It was crazy how quickly Not Your Birthday Birthday had caught on. It was just another one of those things that Harry had helped usher in without asking for acknowledgment or praise.

How did I get such a special young man?

she wondered.

With her eyes locked on her son, she slowly got to her feet and headed inside to start dinner. As the door closed behind her, she heard Harry laughing. It was the sound of a boy trapped between childhood and adulthood —both musical and sad at the same time.

As she headed into the kitchen, feeling rather sad, she heard a whisper. At first, she thought it was nothing. After all, she was the only one in the house. But the voice had been real enough, but incredibly light, almost like a breeze through the house. It made her heart churn and the hairs on her arm stand up.

That soft, still voice said, *Harry will be just fine.*

Startled, Mary Moon looked around the kitchen. As she did, she thought she caught sight of something sitting on the floor by the fridge. But it was not a something. It was a someone. A someone who resembled a rabbit.

The Family Business

She went to the fridge and started dinner while listening to the laughter of the Good Mischief Team through the kitchen window.

Surprise Party

A Spooky Town Bonus Story

M ayor Maximus Kligore hated all birthdays. Especially his own.

He hated the songs, he hated balloons, and he hated the whole idea of getting older. He did like cake. Even the evil mayor of the country's scariest town had his weaknesses and Mayor Kligore's was cake. Especially if it was smothered with strawberry icing.

Today was his birthday. He had heard rumblings there was a surprise party on the way. Oink and Titus had been scheming for two weeks and doing a terrible job of keeping the secret.

Deep down in the hollows of his black and uncaring heart, Kligore knew that this was a frighteningly thoughtful thing for his family and friends to do. And while he did appreciate the effort, the fact that his birthday had come around again made him fitfully angry and terribly sad at the same time.

As the mayor left the We Drive By Night offices and headed home to Folly Farm, he tried to imagine what the surprise party was going to be like. His sons, Titus and Marcus, would be there for sure. Marcus might have his latest girlfriend on his arm. His assistant, Cherry Tomato, would be there, as well as the dark creatures, Oink and Ug. It was a deplorable group of guests for sure, but he guessed it was the closest thing to family he had.

161

Every year when his birthday came around, he did his best not to be overly cranky. It was inevitable, after all; everyone had birthdays, even in a town that was stuck knee-deep in Halloween. With all the goofiness of Sleepy Hollow and its spells and zaniness, the cycle of time still churned on.

He parked his Lustro Phantom inside the twelve-car garage. He made his way to the front door, poking about in the shrubbery and walking around the shadows. He had no intention of being taken by surprise in front of his own home.

Pausing before going inside, he took a deep breath to steady himself. He figured he may as well act surprised. It did mean a lot to him that Titus was behind the party. Sometimes he was worried that Titus would one day leave the family. Dark magic and the family business was not something Titus seemed interested in. His son was the kid with a conscience. Deep down, Titus has a disturbingly good heart. The thought of it made the mayor sad.

162

Kilgore opened the door and prepared to act surprised.

But there was no one there.

The living room was empty. There was not a single creature inside. Not a single present. And certainly not a cake smothered with strawberry icing.

Mayor Kligore walked into his large empty house and was filled with an emotion that he rarely felt. He felt disappointment. He felt . . . sad.

It was odd. He could have sworn he had overheard Titus and Oink whispering about a party from around corners and behind closed doors. He'd even snuck a peek of a text on Titus's phone to Creepy Cakes, the Sleepy Hollow Bakery. Maybe he'd just read things wrong. Maybe he—

SURPRISE!!!

The shouts came from behind him, taking him by surprise and causing him to jump completely off the ground. Somehow, they had managed to all sneak up behind him. They must have circled around through the hallway and quietly moved toward him. Titus, Oink, Ug, Cherry Tomato, and Marcus yelled and shouted and waved balloons. They all grinned at him, but there was also an uncertain look on their faces. It was clear they had been more than a bit worried exactly how the mayor would handle a surprise party.

163

Mayor Kligore rarely smiled, but he couldn't help but let one stretch across his face in that surprised moment. They had really gotten him. He'd *really* been spooked there for a moment. And more than that, he saw that Cherry Tomato was holding a rather large cake, the top of which was coated in thick, rich, strawberry icing.

Oink and Ug carried a few oversize, helium-filled, scary balloons behind their backs as everyone filed into the living room. Mayor Kligore noticed there was no writing or logos or slogans on any of them. There were certainly no numbers on them to indicate his age.

Truthfully, no one knew exactly how old the mayor was—not even Mayor Kligore himself. He was, in a way, ageless. The dark magic that he used so often during the course of his day had taken many things away from him, including the normal processes of aging. Some days, Mayor Kligore wasn't sure if this was a blessing or a curse.

One thing he *did* know was that he had been around for a very long time. The first birthday he could remember having was in a wooded area. He had memories of a Native American girl offering him a cake of bread and a chicken leg as a birthday feast. He had not thought of that girl in quite some time. He tried to remember her name but it was adrift in the clouds of distant memories. Pocahontas, he thought it was.

"You okay, Dad?" Titus asked, putting a hand

on his shoulder.

"Oh, of course," Kligore said. "You all just shocked me. I don't do parties, remember? What were you thinking?"

"Whatever," Marcus said, turning to the rest of the crowd. "I tried to tell you idiots that Dad doesn't like birthdays, much less *birthday parties*."

"Don't be silly," Cherry Tomato said. "Even if he does have something against birthdays, it's nothing a little cake can't fix."

165

Few knew of his secret love for cake, so Mayor Kligore tried to remain calm and slightly bored as Cherry Tomato set the cake down on the kitchen table and started to slice into it.

Oink came over to the mayor, a balloon drifting behind him. "A word, Boss? A word? A word?"

"What is it, slobberboy?" Mayor Kligore grunted.

"Well, sir, I just thought you might like to know that I saw . . . I saw Harry Moon going into Samson

Dupree's magic shop again today. I don't like it when those two spend time together. Don't like it a bit."

"I don't either, Oink. But you know what? Let's not concern ourselves with Harry Moon this evening. It's my birthday, as you all have seen fit to remind me. For a couple of hours, I refuse to worry myself with that little twerp."

"Are you sure, sir? If you don't mind my saying so, you don't look well. Maybe you should go lie down."

"I don't?"

"No, sir. You . . . well, forgive me for saying so, forgive me, but you look . . . *happy.*"

Mayor Kligore took a breath and squinched his face up quickly, making sure that the scowl that usually covered his face was back in place. He hadn't realized that he had slipped into a good mood. He wondered if it had something to do with his birthday or the fact that his family and friends had taken the time and energy to gather together for him.

The longer he ruled over Sleepy Hollow with

evil and greedy power, the more he was learning about the practice of dark magic. No matter how evil someone might be, the sentiment and love of family still got in the way of juicy badness.

The whole idea made him sick to his stomach.

Ug handed him a large slice of cake on a plate as the small group started to sing a very off-key version of *Happy Birthday*. He tolerated it as best as he could, as he believed the Happy Birthday song was legitimately maybe the worst song ever.

"I know you don't do the whole candles thing," Titus announced in front of everyone, "but is there some really big birthday wish you have?"

"I don't waste time with wishes," Kligore said. "Not on falling stars and certainly not on candles on a cake."

"Just pretend, for once," Titus said. "Just for fun."

"Son, I have the dark magic on my side," he

said. "And that is so much better than making some stupid wish on a birthday cake."

"Yeah, but still, Boss Man," Cherry Tomato squealed. "If you had one wish, what would it be?"

The Mayor thought about this for a moment as he finished off his first piece of cake. "You know, I think I'll keep it to myself," he announced. "After all, isn't there some foolish superstition about not telling others what you wish for? If you tell what you wish for, the wish won't come true."

"He's right, he's right," Oink said. "Mum's the word, Boss."

Mayor Kligore scooped up another large piece of cake and looked out of the glass windows on his large French doors. He licked strawberry icing from his fingers, hiding the absolute delight on his face from the others. As he looked out to the east, he could just barely see street lights of Magic Row and a portion of Main Street through these doors. From his second floor study, he could see just about the whole town.

He rolled around the wish in his mind. Although he told Oink that he did not want to think about whatever business Harry Moon was up to, his wish *did* involve the meddlesome little brat.

Because as powerful as the dark magic was, it seemed to have limits when it came to thwarting Harry Moon. So if he could have one wish in his whole entire life, it would be to be rid of Harry once and for all. He wanted that boy, his family, and his close friends out of Sleepy Hollow. And although he had still not come up with an effective way to get that done, he was pretty sure it was just a matter of time.

With a smile and a nod, Mayor Kligore forked up another huge bite of cake.

When it came to getting rid of Harry Moon and having absolute power over Sleepy Hollow, Mayor Kligore felt confident that it would happen quite soon.

He would one day, as the saying went, have his cake and eat it, too.

170

MARK ANDREW POE

The Adventures of Harry Moon author Mark Andrew Poe never thought about being a children's writer growing up. His dream was to love and care for animals, specifically his friends in the rabbit community.

Along the way, Mark became successful in all sorts of interesting careers. He entered the print and publishing world as a young man and his company did really, really well.

Mark became a popular and nationally

NOT YOUR BIRTHDAY BIRTHDAY

sought-after health care advocate for the care and well-being of rabbits.

Years ago, Mark came up with the idea of a story about a young man with a special connection to a world of magic, all revealed through a remarkable rabbit friend. Mark worked on his idea for several years before building a collaborative creative team to help bring his idea to life. And Harry Moon was born.

In 2014, Mark began a multi-book print series project intended to launch *The Adventures of Harry Moon* into the youth marketplace as a hero defined by a love for a magic where love and 'DO NO EVIL' live. Today, Mark continues to work on the many stories of Harry Moon. He lives in suburban Chicago with his wife and his 25 rabbits.

BE SURE TO READ THE CONTINUING AND AMAZING ADVENTURES OF HARRY MOON

The AMAZING Adventures Of

HARRY MOON

Wand - Paper - Scissors

Inspired by true events   Mark Andrew Poe

HARRY MOON is up to his eyeballs in magic in the small town of Sleepy Hollow. His arch enemy, Titus Kligore, has eyes on winning the Annual Scary Talent Show. Harry has a tough job ahead if he is going to steal the crown. He takes a chance on a magical rabbit who introduces him to the deep magic. Harry decides the best way forward is to DO NO EVIL—and the struggle to defeat Titus while winning the affection of the love of his life goes epic.

EVERYONE IS TALKING ABOUT THE ADVENTURES OF HARRY MOON

"After making successful Disney movies like ALADDIN and LITTLE MERMAID, I could never figure out where the magic came from. Now I know. Harry Moon had it all along."

David Kirkpatrick
Former Production Chief, Walt Disney Studios

This may well be one of the most important kid's series in a long time."

- Paul Lewis,
Founder,
Family University
Foundation

"Come on. His name is Harry Moon. How do I not read this?"
- Declan Black
Kid, age 13

"A great coming-of-age book with life principals. Harry Moon is better than Goosebumps and Wimpy Kid. Who'da thunk it?
- Michelle Borquez
Author and Mom

The
AMAZING
Adventures Of

HARRY MOON

Time Machine

Inspired by true events   Mark Andrew Poe

The irrepressible magician of Sleepy Hollow, Harry Moon, sets about to speed up time. Overnight, through some very questionable magic, Harry wishes himself into becoming the high school senior of his dreams. Little did he know that by unleashing time, Harry Moon would come face-to-face with the monster of his worst nightmare. Will Harry find his way home from this supernatural mess?

EVERYONE IS TALKING ABOUT THE ADVENTURES OF HARRY MOON

"Friendship, forgiveness and adventure - Harry Moon will entertain kids and parents alike. My children will have every book in this series on their bookshelf as my gift to them!"

– Regina Jennings
Author and Mom

"Magical and stupendously inspirational, Harry Moon is a hero for the 21st century tween. I wish I had Harry at DISNEY!"

David Kirkpatrick
Former Production Chief, Walt Disney Studios

I can't wait for my next book. Where is the Harry Moon video game?

- Jackson Maison
Kid - age 12

I love my grandchildren and I love Harry Moon. I can't wait to introduce the kids to someone their own age who values life like I do. I hope Harry Moon never ends.

– Scott Hanson
Executive Director, Serve West Dallas
and grandpa

$14.99
ISBN 978-1-943785-04-9

51499>

9 781943 785049

THE AMAZING ADVENTURES OF

HARRY MOON

HALLOWEEN NIGHTMARES

Inspired by true events   Mark Andrew Poe

While other kids are out trick-or-treating, eighth-grade magician Harry Moon is flying on a magic cloak named Impenetrable. Harry and Rabbit speed past severed hands, boiling cauldrons and graveyard witching rituals on their way to unravel a decade old curse at the annual Sleepy Hollow Halloween Bonfire. The sinister Mayor Kligore and Oink are in for the fight of their lives.

EVERYONE IS TALKING ABOUT THE ADVENTURES OF HARRY MOON

"When a character like Harry Moon comes along, you see how important a great story can be to a kid growing up."

- Susan Dawson, Middle School Teacher

"Harry Moon is one wildly magical ride. After making successful films like ALADDIN and LITTLE MERMAID, I wondered where the next hero was coming from Harry Moon has arrived!"

David Kirkpatrick
Former Production Chief, Walt Disney Studios

"A hero with guts who champions truth in the face of great danger. I wish I was thirteen again! If you work with kids, pay attention to Harry Moon."

- Ryan Frank, a Dad and President, KidzMatter

"This is a book I WANT to read."

- Bailey Black
13-Year Old Kid

$14.99
ISBN 978-1-943785-02-5

9 781943 785025

51499>

THE
AMAZING
Adventures Of

HARRY MOON

The Scary Smart House

Inspired by true events   Mark Andrew Poe

When Harry's sister wins a national essay contest in technology, the whole Moon family is treated to a dream weekend in the ultimate, fully loaded, smart house designed by Marvel Modbot, the Walt Disney of the 21st century. It's an incredible blast, with driverless cars and a virtual reality world. That is, until evil thinking invades the smart technology running the smart house, turning that dream tech weekend into an nightmare! The Moons look to Harry and Rabbit to stop the evil before its too late.

EVERYONE IS TALKING ABOUT THE ADVENTURES OF HARRY MOON

"The Moon family's smart house takes on a bone-tingling dimension when the technology that runs it appears haunted. Say hello to SECOS —a scary Smart Evil Central Operating System." –David Kirkpatrick, Former Production Chief, Walt Disney Studios

"I'm a grandpa and Harry Moon is a throw-back to the good old days when kids took on wrong and wrestled it to the ground. My grandkids are getting every book."

– Mark Janes, English and Drama Teacher, Grandfather

"If I was stranded on a desert island, I would want a mat, a pillow, a Harry Moon book and a hatchet."
- Charley, KID, age 11

"I pride myself on never making a bad shot. I focus on perfect form and being rock steady. Like me, Harry Moon delivers under pressure. This kid's my hero."

– Jim Burnworth, Extreme Archer, The Outdoor Channel

$14.99 US / $22.50 CAN
ISBN 978-1-943785-30-8

9 781943 785308

The

THE
AMAZING
ADVENTURES OF

HARRY MOON

HAUNTED PIZZA

Inspired by true events   Mark Andrew Poe

The new Pizza Slice is doing booming business, but the kids in Sleepy Hollow Middle School are transforming into strange creatures the more they eat of the haunted cheesy delicacy. Even the Good Mischief Team are falling under the spell of the new haunted pizza slices, putting Harry and his magic Rabbit on the scent to the truth behind the peperoni mystery.

EVERYONE IS TALKING ABOUT THE ADVENTURES OF HARRY MOON

"The Moon family's smart house takes on a bone-tingling dimension when the technology that runs it appears haunted. Say hello to SECOS –a scary Smart Evil Central Operating System!" –David Kirkpatrick, Former Production Chief, Walt Disney Studios

"I'm a grandpa and Harry Moon is a throw-back to the good old days when kids took on wrong and wrestled it to the ground. My grandkids are getting every book."

– Mark Janes, English and Drama Teacher, Grandfather

"If I was stranded on a desert island, I would want a mat, a pillow, a Harry Moon book and a hatchet" – Charley, KID, age 11

"I pride myself on never making a bad shot. I focus on perfect form and being rock steady. Like me, Harry Moon delivers under pressure. This kid's my hero."

– Jim Burnworth, Extreme Archer, The Outdoor Channel

THE ENCHANTED WORLD OF HONEY MOON

MOUNTAIN MAYHEM

Suzanne Brooks Kuhn   Created by Mark Andrew Poe

Hit the trail girls! It's on to the Appalachian Trail. Honey and the Spooky Scouts set off on a mountain trek to earn their final Mummy Mates patch. But an inept troop leader, a flash flood and a campfire catastrophe threaten to keep them from reaching the Sleepy Hollow finish line in time. When all seems lost, Honey Moon takes charge and nothing will stop her from that final patch!

"Honey is a bit of magical beauty...adventure and brains rolled into one."
David Kirkpatrick, Former Production Chief, Walt Disney Studios

"Magic, mystery and a little mayhem. Three things that make a story great. Honey Moon is a great story."
-- Dawn Moore
Life Coach and Educator

"A wonderful experience for girls looking for a new hero. I think her name is Honey Moon." - Nancy Dimes, Teacher & Mom

"I absolutely cannot wait to begin my next adventure with Honey Moon. I love her"
– Carly Wujcik, Kid, age 11

"Charm, wit and even a bit of mystery. Honey Moon is a terrific piece of writing that will keep kids asking for more."
--Priscilla Strapp, Writer, Foster Mom

$14.99 US / $22.50 CAN

9 781943 785186

90000>

THE ENCHANTED WORLD OF HONEY MOON

SHADES AND SHENANIGANS

Suzanne Brooks Kuhn   Created by Mark Andrew Poe

When Honey comes face-to-face with
Clarice Kligore and her Royal Shades
she knows something must be done to
keep this not very nice club from
taking over Sleepy Hollow Elementary.
Honey sets out to beat them at their
own game by forming her own club,
The Queen Bees. Instead of chasing the
Shades off the playground for good,
Honey learns that being the Queen Bee
is more about the honey than the sting.

"Honey goes where she is needed . . . and everyone needs Honey Moon!"
— David Kirkpatrick, Former Production Chief, Walt Disney Studios

"I wish Honey Moon had been written when
my girls were young. She would have charmed
her way into their hearts."
- Nora Wolfe, Mother of Two

"Heart, humor, age-
appropriate puppy love
and wisdom. Honey's
not perfect but she is
striving to be a good,
strong kid."
— Anne Brighen
Elementary School Teacher

"My favorite character of
all time. I love Honey."
- Elise Rogers, Age 9

"I am a grandmother. I knew ahead of time that these books were
aimed at younger readers but I could not resist and thank goodness
for that! A great kid's book!"
--Carri Zimmerman, Grandmother of Twelve

$14.99
ISBN 978-1-943785-16-2
51499>

9 781943 785162

THE ENCHANTED WORLD OF HONEY MOON

NOT YOUR VALENTINE

Regina Jennings   Created by Mark Andrew Poe

A Sleepy Hollow Valentine's Day dance with a boy! NO WAY, NO HOW is Honey Moon going to a scary sweetheart dance with that Noah kid. But, after being forced to dance together in PE class, word gets around that Honey likes Noah. Now, she has no choice but to stop Valentine's Day in its tracks. Things never go as planned and Honey winds up with the surprise of her Sleepy Hollow life.

"Honey is a breakout wonder... What a pint-sized powerhouse!"
- David Kirkpatrick, Former Production Chief, Walt Disney Studios

"A dance, a boy and Honey Moon - every girl wants to know how this story will end up."
- Deby Less, Mom and Teacher

"What better way to send a daughter off to sleep than knowing she can conquer any problem by doing the right thing."
- Jean Zyskowski
Mom and Office Manager

"I love to read and Honey Moon is my favorite of all!"
- Lilah Black, KID age 8

"Makes me want to have daughters again so they could grow up with Honey Moon. Strong and vulnerable heroines make raising healthy children even more exciting.
--Suzanne Kuhn, Best-selling Author Coach

$14.99
ISBN 978-1-943785-08-7

51499>

9 781943 785087